THE NIGHT BEFORE FIFTH GRADE.

"Help me, girl," I whispered when she sniffed up over the edge of the mattress.

She couldn't hear me even if I'd shouted, so I whispered again, "I mean it—help me. Please." Maxi put her front paws on the mattress and looked at me. The full moon glowed through the skylight directly above my bed.

Maxi stared at me, deep, past my eyes, to the inside.

"I need you," I whispered, or maybe I only thought it.

Maxi never took her eyes from mine as she backed up, then leaped forward onto my bed for the first time by herself. She nudged the twisted covers and somehow released them, freeing me from being a bed mummy. Then she pressed her head into my chest, giving me a Maxi hug.

"Thank you, girl. I needed that."

Her head tilted and she lapped my face. Then she curled up next to me and laid her head on my chest, pushing down ever so gently, every few seconds, gently, slowly, slowly, gently—changing my breaths from short pants to calming sighs.

"Maybe, just maybe I can do this, girl. If you say so."

SECRET #8
It's possible to hear someone even if your ears don't work.

OTHER BOOKS YOU MAY ENJOY

MAXI'S SECRETS

(OR, WHAT YOU CAN LEARN FROM A DOG)

LYNN PLOURDE

PUFFIN BOOKS

PUFFIN BOOKS
An imprint of Penguin Random House LLC
375 Hudson Street
New York, New York 10014

First published in the United States of America by Nancy Paulsen Books, 2016
Published by Puffin Books, an imprint of Penguin Random House LLC, 2017

THE LIBRARY OF CONGRESS HAS CATALOGED THE NANCY PAULSEN BOOKS EDITION AS FOLLOWS:
Names: Plourde, Lynn, author.
Title: Maxi's secrets : (or what you can learn from a dog) / Lynn Plourde.
Description: New York, NY : Nancy Paulsen Books, [2016]
Summary: "Fifth-grader Timminy, who's small for his age and new in town, isn't eager to
start middle school—but he gets a great consolation prize in Maxi, a big, deaf, lovable dog"—
Provided by publisher. Identifiers: LCCN 2016003361 | ISBN 9780399545672 (hardback)
Subjects: | CYAC: Size—Fiction. | Dogs—Fiction. | Friendship—Fiction. | Middle schools—Fiction.
| Schools—Fiction. | BISAC: JUVENILE FICTION / Animals / Dogs. | JUVENILE FICTION /
Social Issues / Friendship. | JUVENILE FICTION / Social Issues / Special Needs.
Classification: LCC PZ7.P724 Max 2016 | DDC [Fic]—dc23
LC record available at https://lccn.loc.gov/2016003361

Puffin Books ISBN 9780399545689

Printed in the United States of America

5 7 9 10 8 6

Design by Annie Ericsson
Chapter opener art © Maira Kalman

For Maggie, my inspiration,
and Paul, my believer

CHAPTER 1

LET'S GET THIS part over with—it's no secret.

My dog, Maxi, dies.

Just like Old Yeller, Sounder, Old Dan, and Little Ann all died. Except those dogs were fictional. You cried, I cried when fake dogs died. Maxi was *real*.

So real, I can still sniff and get a whiff of her stinky dog breath—even though she's been gone for fifty-two days now. Maybe it's because I haven't vacuumed a single strand of the white fur coat she left behind. And when your dog is a giant, that's enough fur to cover a baby polar bear. Her dried dog slobber is everywhere too—like a hundred tattoos she branded my room with so I wouldn't forget her.

No way I'd forget her.

I swear some nights I still hear Maxi nudging my bedroom door coming in to check on me after checking the rest of the house. With her guard duties done, she can plop down on my mattress. My mattress that's still on the floor because she couldn't climb up in bed with me anymore so I moved it down to her level.

But when I wake confused and open the door to let her in, there's just emptiness. Emptiness that I rush to shut out, but I can't. Emptiness slips under the covers with me. Emptiness is cold, not dog-warm. Emptiness is silent, not dog-snoring. Emptiness stinks worse than a dog's breath. Emptiness stinks so bad it can suffocate you.

But you can't let it.

When I start to breathe again, I realize *having* Maxi in my life will always be a bigger deal than *losing* Maxi. Her tail still thump-thump-thumps in my heart.

And that crazy dog taught me so much. You won't believe all the secrets she shared with me. Plus some other secrets she helped me dig up, deeper than buried bones, inside myself. And sniff out still more secrets from others.

Except, they're *not* secrets anymore since I'm telling *you*. That's okay 'cause Maxi would want you to know. She'd bark them to the world if she could.

If she were still here.

SECRET #1
You can learn a lot from a dog you love.

CHAPTER 2

TO BE HONEST, I never dreamed of getting a dog. Maxi was a bribe from my parents.

"We know you don't like the idea of moving, Timminy, but Skenago is out in the country. So guess what?" My mom looked at my dad, as if they'd rehearsed this, and he chimed in with her: "You can have a dog!"

I folded my arms. "No, thanks. I'll stay here in Portland, in our apartment. You two can move to Skenago and get a dog to keep you company. I'm *not* going."

Yup. Even as a fourth grader, I was lippy. That happens when you're short—you're always trying to find ways to sound and act bigger.

My parents usually called me out for being a wisemouth, but I knew they wouldn't that time because they wanted me to move more than they wanted me to shut my trap.

It worked. They won. The landlord wouldn't take my

piggybank for rent money so we *all* moved to the house in the country. I hated moving, although Maxi was the ultimate consolation prize. Besides, the busy streets of Portland would have been dangerous for a dog like Maxi.

I'm not sure Maxi ever realized she was deaf—not once in her whole short life. We didn't notice when we first got her, and by the time we figured it out, it didn't matter.

My parents didn't return me to Maine Med where I was born when they realized years later that I took after my great-great-uncle Lex and was short—*really, really* short—in the 0.001 percentile of height for kids my age. (Notice I said *kids*—I'm not just short for boys my age, but girls too.) Poor Great-great-uncle Lex owned a meat market and had to stand on a wooden crate to see over the counter to wait on his customers. You'll be glad to know I've already crossed butcher off my future-dream-jobs list.

No, if my parents didn't bring me back to the hospital when they found out what was wrong with me, I wouldn't bring Maxi back to the breeder's just because she was deaf.

Actually, the first time I met Maxi, I didn't notice anything different about her. And I don't think she noticed anything different about me either.

My parents and I stepped inside the circular wire fence for a closer look at the seven pups for sale in the litter. One puppy began circling *me*, keeping the others away. I scooped it up—nose to snout—

and . . .

Smooch! Slurp!

"This is the one," I told my parents.

"But what about one of the boys?" Dad asked.

"Dad, I'm your boy. Time to mix things up with a girl."

"Are you sure? This is the first puppy ad we've answered," Mom whispered so the breeder wouldn't hear. "And we have three more places to check. Maybe we should see those first."

Maxi wouldn't stop licking me.

"She's crazy about me, Mom."

"But some of the other breeds we're looking at are . . . different . . . they're not quite as . . . um . . ."

"Spit it out, Mom—BIG! The other breeds aren't as big as Great Pyrenees. You're worried your puppy will grow up to be bigger than your son."

"I was going to say white, Timminy. It'll be hard to keep a white dog clean."

I made Mom a bunch of kid promises. "I'll give her a bath twice a week. I'll brush her teeth so you can't tell where her white fur ends and her white teeth begin."

Then I really piled it on. "Puhleeeeeeeeeeeeeeeeeeeeeeeeeeeeease! You moved me to this new town where I'm all alone and have no friends. This pup is all I've got."

Dad looked at Mom. "Give it up, Lynda. You've already lost this one."

"Thanks, Dad," I said, grateful that I didn't have to turn on the tears. I would have if I had to.

After they paid and we were loading Maxi (Maxi—who didn't have the name Maxi yet, but I can't call her *it*, can I?) into our car, Dad opened the back hatch.

"I'll hold her in the backseat with me," I said.

"No, Timminy. She's going back here in the crate we brought."

"That's mean, Dad. Look, she's shivering. She's never been away from her pack before. If I hold her, she'll know she still has a pack, just a new one."

Mom piped in, "But what if she does her 'business' in the car?"

"She won't. Let's see if she has to go now. And if she still goes in the car, I'll clean it up."

My parents looked skeptical but didn't say anything as I led Maxi around the breeder's yard with a leash. Actually, *she* led me around the yard as she stopped to sniff every two feet . . .

two feet, sniff,

two feet, sniff-sniff,

two feet, sniff-sniff-sniff,

two feet, sniff-sniff-sniff-sniff-squat-pee.

Success! I was prouder than the first time I peed by myself on the potty chair.

"See, Mom."

I climbed into the backseat with Maxi.

"Lynda?" Dad looked at Mom for permission to drive off.

"Kenneth?" Mom threw the question right back at him.

"Oh, okay," he said with a sigh. "Are you buckled up back there?"

"The two-legged one is buckled. Not sure how to buckle the four-legged one."

Dad gave me one of *those* looks in the rearview mirror. I shut my trap before he decided to put me in the crate.

As we headed home, the more Maxi quivered, the tighter I held her. I was hoping she'd doze off, but instead she started whining. So I held her even tighter. Too tight, I guess. Squeezed something right out of her.

I froze, hoped no one would notice.

But Mom sniffed and looked at Dad. "Kenneth, is that you?"

"Not me," said Dad.

"Kenneth?" She didn't believe him. Whenever Dad cuts the cheese, he always denies it and says, "First one who smelt it must have dealt it."

When Dad didn't give his "smelt it" line, Mom realized he wasn't the one who dealt it.

"Timminy!" they both shouted.

"Wasn't me."

"The puppy!" My parents were getting good at talking in unison.

"Why don't they make diapers for puppies?" I asked. "After all, they're *babies*."

SECRET #2

Sometimes love stinks.

CHAPTER 3

SO HOW DID Maxi end up with the name Maxi?

First, you have to know my dad has always been the namer in our family. It wasn't a male-dominance kind of thing for Dad. "Ugh! Me Kenneth, me nameth." Nah! It's just he really likes naming things. He is into genealogy and a lifetime member of ancestry.com. I may not like the names my dad comes up with, but I've gotta give him credit for being the hardest-working namer I know.

Take my name, Timminy. Dad wanted to honor our families when he named me so he studied his and Mom's family trees. He should have saved himself some work and named me Great-great-uncle Lex the Second—except he didn't know then I'd grow up to be a shorty. After all, all babies are short. They're measured in inches!

He decided in the end to call me Timminy in honor of two great-great-grandfathers. On Mom's side, my great-great-grandfather was Timotheus, a preacher, whose name meant "valued by God." Maybe Dad thought he'd be guaranteeing me a ticket to heaven with that part of my name. The other part was from Dad's side, my great-great-grandfather Minyamin, which meant "right-hand son." I'm left-handed, which Dad didn't know when I was a baby.

So in the end, half of TIMotheus plus half of MINYamin equals TIMMINY. That's me.

When you have a name no one has heard before, you're called other things . . . TimOTHy (even when teachers read it on their class lists, they usually say OTH instead of IN—and they're supposed be teaching *me* how to read). Some shorten it to Timmi (a little too cutesy for my taste with that *i* at the end). And then there's the nickname Minny. I didn't mind Minny when I was young, but for a kid my size it stinks big-time now (bigger even than Maxi stinks when she does her business).

But enough about me. What about Maxi's name? Dad was determined to name her Maxine after my great-great-aunt Maxine, who owned twenty-three dogs at one time.

I protested, "Dad, you can't name this puppy Maxine."

"Maxine it is," Dad said. "I've researched carefully. Great-great-aunt Maxine would be most honored—God rest her soul."

"Dad, this puppy would be most embarrassed—God wouldn't stick her with a name that *old*. What will the other puppies in the neighborhood think?"

"I've made up my mind, Timminy."

I didn't fight him. I just started calling her Maxi.

When Dad said, "But her name's really Maxine," I answered, "Yeah, but she doesn't look like a Maxine yet—we can call her that when she's an old girl. Maxi is a good nickname for a puppy."

Of course, I had no way of knowing then that Maxi would never get to be an old girl.

I also had no way of knowing then that it didn't matter what we called her—Maxine, Maxi, Backseat Pooper—since she never once heard us say her name.

SECRET #3

Sometimes all the energy you put into something you think matters doesn't matter one bit.

CHAPTER 4

SO HOW LONG did it take us to realize Maxi was deaf?

Longer than you'd think.

We were busy unpacking from our move and checking out our new town. Skenago's corner store sold more than fifty flavors of homemade fudge and there was a drive-in movie theater—none of us had ever been to a drive-in, so we went twice in one week and saw the same movie.

Plus we were puppy newbies and busy with all that feeding-walking-peeing-pooping stuff. It's not easy. I gained new respect for Great-great-aunt Maxine, the Queen of Canines. How'd she handle twenty-three dogs at once? I could hardly handle one.

Take Maxi out—nothing happens.

Take Maxi back out—nothing happens.

Take Maxi back out again—nothing happens.

Take Maxi in—SOMETHING!

Poor Great-great-aunt Maxine! That must have been something to take care of all those dogs' somethings!

Besides figuring out Maxi's bathroom schedule, I tried to learn all I could about her breed. Great Pyrenees were bred to guard livestock and make sure no big bad wolves snuck up at night and got them. Poor Maxi! Dad, Mom, and I were her only livestock. She'd try to gather us into one room so we'd be easier to guard, but we weren't very cooperative. I'd be playing games in my room, Mom would be reading in her room, Dad would be watching the History Channel in the living room, and Maxi would be roaming room to room to room.

Sometimes, we'd yell, "Pig pile," and run and crash on Dad. Then Maxi only had to walk around and around the couch to keep us safe from those big bad wolves. Good girl!

Great Pyrenees are also supersmart. Just what I, a smarty-pants, deserved. They were bred to think for themselves. That's why it takes them longer to learn to follow commands.

We also didn't know anyone else with a Pyr (that's the short name for Great Pyrenees) to compare our experiences with. I read stuff online, the vet told us more stuff, but the best place was the "I Love Great Pyrenees" Facebook page. Dad found it and shared their posts with me
    Every.

Single.

Day.

(Don't tell Dad, but I'm glad he did. It was sort of like our own Secret Dog Club.)

"Jiminy cricket, Timminy, take a gander at this one."

Poor Dad! Still stuck in Pinocchio Land talking about Jiminy Cricket. And who uses the word *gander*? My dad does. If you bothered to ask him (what was I thinking!), he'd say, "*Gander*, as a verb, has American origins, around 1900, and came from the idea of a male goose stretching its long neck to get a better look at something."

So I took a gander over Dad's shoulder. "Wow! Look at that one." The Facebook photo showed a giant Pyr sitting on a woman's lap with the words *My baby!*

"It seems all Pyrs, no matter their size, think they're lapdogs." Dad laughed, then pointed. "Check out the comments. Everyone's saying how much their Pyrs weigh . . . 146 pounds . . . 151 . . ."

I jumped in. "This one's only 109 pounds. But that one says 139, 183, 164. Yikes—192!"

"Don't tell your mother. She doesn't need to know how big Maxi might get."

Just then Mom walked by. "Don't tell me what?" she asked.

"Nothing, Lynda," said Dad. "A guy secret."

Mom sighed, patted Maxi, who was lying at Dad's feet,

and said, "Well then, Maxi and I won't tell you our gal secret—that the average adult female Pyr weighs eighty-five to a hundred fifteen pounds and gains up to ten pounds a month during the first year. But, *shhhhh*, Maxi, don't yip a word of it to the guys." Mom walked off.

"How does she do that, Timminy? How does your mom get me every single time?"

"Um . . . Dad, you forget moms have eyes in the backs of their heads, plus it looks to me like you leave the door wide-open for her to walk right in and get you

Every.

Single.

Time."

"Come on, Maxi." Dad tugged on her collar. "Let's go for a walk. You're the only one in this house who doesn't give me any lip."

SECRET #4

Something can stare you in the face and you *still* can't see it. Better take another gander.

CHAPTER 5

"IS THIS PART of our property?" I asked Dad as we headed into the woods behind our house.

"No, we have three acres. This is a public recreation area that anyone can use for hiking, snowshoeing, or whatever. This way, Timminy. I think the trail starts by that giant white pine up ahead."

Dad was right. A trail wide enough for us to walk side by side zigzagged through the woods. It was easy to follow. Instead of a yellow brick road, it was a carpet of decayed leaves from last fall that shuffled under our feet.

The shade was refreshing, nature's air conditioner on a hot summer day. Splatters of sunlight shimmered through the trees. And Maxi was in scent heaven as her snout sniffed every dead leaf and hidden plop of animal poop. We walked and walked and didn't talk for the longest time.

Until finally, I let out the biggest sigh and said, "It's nice . . . really nice out here. Much quieter than walking Back Cove in Portland with all the city sounds."

"Yeah, a nice place to escape," Dad said. "We might need it."

"What do you mean?"

"School starts in two weeks. Are you ready?"

"The question is—are *you* ready, Dad?"

"Sure, a little nervous though."

"You should be! Being an assistant principal is going to be a lot tougher than being a teacher. And I heard everyone hates assistant principals."

"Gee, Timminy, way to make your old man feel better about starting his first administrative job. Does that mean you're going to hate me too?"

"Nope. We know who buys the dog food around here. Don't we, Maxi?"

Maxi didn't notice I'd said her name. But why should she? She was busy slurping from a puddle.

"I don't know why they put fifth grade in their middle school up here."

"I told you small towns group grades differently," Dad said. "They don't have as many students or schools as a city so you're stuck with me at the middle school."

"It's not you I'm worried about, Dad. Do you know how *big* eighth graders grow? Bigger than you! Heck, if there's another shrimpy kid like me, one of those eighth graders could grab us, one in each hand, and jam us into the same locker. And we'd fit!"

Dad peered over his glasses. "That's not going to happen, Timminy. You're letting your imagination run wild again."

"You're right, Dad. That won't happen."

"Glad you're coming to your senses."

"Me too. What was I thinking? There's no way there will be another kid as short as me at Skenago Middle School—unless they go across town and steal a kindergartener from the elementary school. That eighth grader will only have *me* to stuff into a locker with enough room left over for sports equipment."

Dad shook his head.

I continued, "I've been thinking. Maybe fifth grade is the perfect year for homeschooling."

"And who's going to teach you? I'll be at the middle school, and your mom is starting her new speech therapy job at the Head Start."

"Maxi! Maxi will teach me. Won't you, girl?" I grabbed Maxi's leash from Dad and raced ahead. "Come on, Maxi, whatcha gonna teach me?"

"Timminy! You can't run away from your problems."

"I can try," I shouted back at him. I let Maxi off her leash and said, "Let's run away together, girl. You're bigger than Toto, but follow the leaf trail and show me the way to Munchkin Land, where I'll fit right in."

Maxi raced ahead. Even her puppy legs were faster than my short legs.

"Catch her," Dad yelled after me. "We don't know where these trails go."

I sprinted after her.

Woof-woof! I heard Maxi up ahead. Had she found Munchkin Land already?

I ran faster, stopped, and laughed. Dad caught up and started laughing too.

Maxi had treed a squirrel. She raced around and around the base of the tree as if she were a merry-go-round animal. We couldn't tell if she thought the squirrel was new livestock to guard or an enemy wolf-squirrel she was protecting us from. Either way, I got dizzy watching her.

That's when we heard it.

Vroom-vroom-vroom!

What sounded like an engine echoed through the trees, louder and louder and louder. I looked around and saw nothing. Then I glanced up. Couldn't be a chopper, could it?

Dad shouted and pointed, "THERE!"

We dove out of the way just as a four-wheeling ATV raced around the bend.

"Hey!" the driver yelled. "You almost made me crash."

"Slow down!" Dad hollered over the engine. "You almost crashed into us!"

"Jerk!" I yelled, crawling out of the bushes where I'd landed.

The driver killed the engine, jumped off his machine, and shoved a finger in my face, my face that was slightly above his belly button. "Who you calling a jerk, shrimp?"

Dad stepped between us. "Calm down, everyone."

I turned my glare from the Jerk to Dad. What did he mean by *everyone*? There was only one jerk here. Why'd Dad choose this second to start practicing his assistant principal skills? I needed him to be a dad and stand up for his son and his poor defenseless puppy.

"Maxi!" I gasped, remembering she was still off her leash. She must have been scared to death. Where'd she gone during all the commotion?

The Jerk turned and looked where I was looking. "Aww!" he said. "What a cute puppy! Better keep her on a leash, though, to be safe out here."

"Yeah, thanks to *some* people it's not safe!"

Dad gave me one of those leave-it-alone looks.

I had no choice. With the Jerk and Dad, two against one, I didn't stand a chance. Besides, I was more concerned about Maxi, who was still on her squirrel mission as if nothing had happened.

"You okay, girl?"

Maxi didn't look at me, didn't look at any of us.

Dad slipped her leash back on and tugged her toward us.

That's when she saw the Jerk, wagged her tail, and licked his hand.

Now it was *three* against one.

"What kind of dog?" asked the Jerk.

"A Great Pyrenees," answered Dad.

"Whoa! Aren't those the kind that grow big, really big?"

Dad nodded. "She'll probably get to be about a hundred pounds."

"Hey, you'll be able to ride her for a pony, kid." He snorted at his own joke.

Before I could say anything, Dad nudged me back toward home.

"See you around," he said. "Oh, and please slow down. We're new to the neighborhood and our puppy likes going for walks on these trails."

"Gotcha. I'll keep an eye out for the Little Beast."

My throat clenched, and I let out a low growl.

Dad nudged me again and whispered, "Keep walking. Just keep walking."

As the Jerk revved his engine and drove off—a little slower (maybe by *two* miles per hour)—I growled louder. "Ooooh, he's the beast! And why didn't you stick up for me, Dad?"

"Let it go, Timminy. We'll probably never see him again."

"Dad, he obviously lives in this neighborhood. Do

you think he's from a street gang in Portland and followed us up here? We'll see him again, probably at our school!"

Dad swallowed hard. "Nah! He's big enough to be in high school."

"Oh, Dad, high school kids ride motorcycles on *real* roads, not ATVs on trails. Eighth graders grow big, *really* big!"

Woof! Maxi barked to get us moving again. It was almost suppertime.

"Coming, girl," Dad said.

As we walked back, Dad and I fell silent again. But we weren't lost in the peace and beauty of the woods anymore. And we weren't even thinking about the Jerk anymore.

No, this time we both stared at Maxi. How could she have missed all that commotion?

SECRET #5
The truth can't stay a secret forever.

CHAPTER 6

WHEN WE GOT HOME, Mom had Maxi's food waiting in her dish. Dad and I just stared as she ate.

"What's up?" asked Mom.

I started, "Maxi . . . out there . . . the loudest ATV engine in the world, louder than a jet engine—"

"Not that loud," Dad jumped in. "But really close to us and loud. And Maxi didn't—"

"No, she didn't," I agreed.

"Spit it out. She didn't what?" asked Mom.

Dad and I shouted, "HEAR!"

We filled Mom in. Dad played down the we-almost-got-crushed-by-the-ATV part and I played up the big-jerk part.

"Were you looking at her when the ATV approached?" asked Mom.

"*Approached* isn't the right word, Mom. It *zoomed*! And we were just trying not to get kill—"

Dad cut me off: "We were busy getting out of the way of the four-wheeler, so, no, we weren't watching Maxi and her reaction."

"But she never noticed, Mom. She was still after that squirrel."

"Maybe she was too distracted by the squirrel."

"Maybe," I said. I wanted to believe Maxi could hear.

"Help me finish getting supper ready, you two," said Mom. "Then while we're eating we can come up with a strategy to figure out if Maxi is really deaf, only hearing-impaired, or if it's just your vivid imaginations."

After supper, Dad and I did research while Mom tested Maxi. We found a Facebook page called "Deaf Dogs Rock." We already knew Maxi rocked whether she was deaf or not. But when we clicked on their website and links, we discovered that more white dogs were born deaf than any other color—it's some sort of genetic, pigment thing.

"But not *all* white dogs are deaf, right?" I asked.

Dad nodded, but his nod wasn't very reassuring.

Dad and I peeked in on Mom, who sat in the recliner while Maxi dozed on her bed by the sliding glass doors. Mom had her phone open to the ringtones app. At random intervals, Mom tried different ringtones—but Maxi's only actions were dream twitches.

Except the one time she jumped up and barked at a squirrel on the other side of the sliding doors. But had she heard the drumming ringtone right before she woke up and saw the squirrel? Or maybe her strong sniffer had smelled the squirrel through the door and that woke her up. Or maybe this was a dumb experiment. Maxi had never reacted when phones rang. Most dogs don't— they're dogs! Who's gonna call a dog?

Our opinion would change every day, sometimes hourly . . .

"She's *not* deaf," I declared when Maxi raced into the kitchen as I microwaved popcorn.

"Try again, Sherlock Holmes," answered Dad. "Remember that a dog's sense of smell is thousands of times more powerful than a human's. She didn't hear the popcorn popping. She smelled it and hoped you'd share. Heck, even I smelled it with my inferior nose from the den—with the door closed! Why do you think I'm here? Gonna share that popcorn with your favorite father?"

Whenever Maxi was left home alone in her crate while we were away, she'd start barking as soon as one of us walked through the door. But did she hear the door? Hear us holler her name? Or did she somehow notice a change in light or air pressure when the door opened?

Or maybe it was in Maxi's blood not to listen? A lot of owners on the "I Love Great Pyrenees" Facebook page complained their Pyr puppies were so stubborn, were such independent thinkers, that they would have sworn they were deaf.

We were stumped. Was Maxi deaf, or acting like a typical Pyr pup? So we made Maxi an appointment with a veterinary specialist in Portland for the next week. Maybe then we'd finally get an answer.

SECRET #6
Life is never black or white—even if you're a WHITE Great Pyrenees.

CHAPTER 7

THE TWO-HOUR TRIP to the vet's in Portland was going to be the longest car ride Maxi had taken.

I climbed into the backseat, buckled up, and spent the first twenty minutes with my head turned toward Maxi in her crate in the back while repeating, "It's okay, girl. I'm right here. Don't worry. It's okay, girl. I'm right here. Don't worry. It's okay, girl. I'm . . ."

Mom cleared her throat.

". . . right here. Don't worry. It's okay . . ."

Mom cleared her throat louder.

When I turned toward the front, she gazed at me in the rearview mirror and pulled her fingers across her lips . . . I nodded, zipped my lips, and all I could hear was . . .

Maxi snoring.

I smiled. "Guess my talking calmed her down and put her to sleep, Mom."

"Timminy, we're on our way to find out if Maxi's

deaf. She may not have heard anything you said. Lucky her, because your talking gave me a headache."

"Sorry."

I leaned my head against the window watching the blur of green as we headed south on I-95. Growing up in the city, I wasn't sure how to tell oaks from maples from ash trees, but I did know pine trees, so I should thank whoever decided to call Maine the Pine Tree State.

After a half hour, Maxi was still snoring and Mom looked calmer so I asked, "How are they gonna figure out if Maxi's deaf?"

"I'm not a hundred percent sure. But I was reading up on it, and it sounds like they'll do a BAER test."

"Yikes! A *bear* test? Growling? What if it scares her?"

"Not that kind of bear, Timminy. But it is pronounced the same way. Reverse the vowels. It's B-A-E-R and stands for Brainstem Auditory Evoked Response. Basically, they hook wires up to dogs' ears, play sounds at different loudness and pitch levels, and watch a computer to see if the dogs' brains register that they're hearing the sounds."

"So Maxi doesn't have to do anything?"

"Nope. They use the BAER on human babies, too, to figure out if they're deaf. Maxi might not be deaf-deaf. She might be hearing-impaired and be able to hear some sounds, like high-pitched or low-pitched ones. Any hearing would be good and could help keep her safe."

I spent the rest of the ride mouthing the words, *Hear*

the BAER growl, Maxi. Hear the BAER growl, Maxi.
Hear the BAER growl, Maxi.

When we arrived at the vet's, Maxi lunged forward on her leash as Mom tried to hold her back. She was determined to inspect the scent of every dog, cat, rabbit, gerbil, hamster, and guinea pig that had ever set paws in that vet's office. Most people in the waiting room "aww-ed" over her. But one lady with two cat carriers tsk-tsked, "Get that big thing away from my little princesses."

Mom said, "She's just curious."

Still, a vet assistant whisked us into a room and said, "Dr. Davis will be with you shortly."

"Maxi," I said, "how's it feel to have someone think you're too big? That's never happened to me. You're making me jealous, girl. Promise you won't ever become a *princess*."

Dr. Davis came in then. Maxi went right up to her, sniffing her white coat. As she patted Maxi with one hand, she put a finger up to her lips signaling Mom and me to be quiet. A door behind us opened and the vet assistant stepped back into the room. She said, "Maxi. *Maxi. MAXI,*" louder and louder and louder each time. Maxi didn't notice. She just kept sniffing and getting pats from Dr. Davis. Then the assistant shook a can full of coins. Maxi still didn't react. Finally, the assistant blew a whistle. I couldn't hear the whistle so no wonder Maxi didn't notice that one.

"She's deaf," Dr. Davis said.

Mom asked, "Are you sure?"

"Yes."

I jumped in. *Someone* had to defend Maxi. "But I didn't hear the whistle. You can't expect Maxi to hear that thing."

Dr. Davis looked right at me. "Yes, I can—it's an ultrasound whistle that's so high-pitched dogs can hear it, but humans can't. She didn't hear her name, the low-pitched coins, the high-pitched whistle—none of it." Dr. Davis turned toward Mom and continued, "I could give her the BAER test to prove it to you, but that's expensive. There's no need. Sorry."

I didn't hear anything after "sorry."

She wasn't as sorry as I was.

Maxi didn't deserve to be deaf. She never did anything to anyone. She was an innocent puppy.

Poor Maxi. She'd never hear my dad's sneezes that could wake a dead person. She'd never hear my mom sing Elton John songs off-key while she vacuumed. She'd never hear me say, "I love you, girl." I wanted to shout the whole two-hour ride back home, "Life's not fair! Life's not fair! Life's not fair!"

But instead I was silent.

Just like Maxi's world—silent.

SECRET #7
Bad news is still bad news—even if you're expecting it.

CHAPTER 8

MAXI WAS DEAF.

DEAF.

In a way, it was a relief to know. I could stop worrying she *might be* deaf and start dealing with the reality — she *was* deaf. I couldn't wish it away no matter how hard I tried. Like it never worked when I tried to wish away being short. (Those blowing-out-birthday-candles and first-star-I-see-tonight wishes are a joke. If I'm ever a parent, I'll tell my kids, "There are some things you can't change, kids, so don't even bother trying. Toughen up and get used to them.")

It didn't work to wish away school either. But why did it have to start in August? I wasn't ready. Whose idea was it to steal kids' summer vacation? In Portland, school had always started in September, after Labor Day. Dad had no reasonable answer — just that schools in this part of Maine were *different*. I was sick of different. My whole life was about being different.

"Do you want to ride to school with me tomorrow or take the bus?" asked Dad. "I'm going in extra early since it's the first student day."

"How early?"

"Leaving here at six fifteen."

"Ouch! Maybe I'll take the bus."

"Okay," said Dad.

"But I won't know anybody. Even worse, the Jerk might be on the bus . . . if he doesn't ride his four-wheeler to school. If he does, maybe he'll give me a ride on the back."

"Timminy . . ." Dad didn't say any more. He didn't need to.

"I'll sleep on it and let you know in the morning."

"But—" Dad started.

"I know, I know. If I'm riding with you, I have to be in the car at six fifteen sharp."

"You got it," said Dad. "Or *vroom-vroom*—my four-wheeler leaves without you."

He smiled at his attempt at a joke. I didn't.

That night I tossed and turned until the sheets and blankets were twisted into a knot with me tied in the middle.

I forced myself to lie still and take a few deep breaths. I knew I wouldn't die if I didn't get any sleep. I'd never gotten much sleep the nights before the first day of school. In kindergarten, first, and second grade, it was because I was anxious. Good anxious.

In third and fourth grade, I was anxious too. Bad anxious. By then I'd figured out other kids grew a lot over the summer. So even if I stayed the same height, it actually seemed like I'd shrunk. The short digs from the other kids started on the first day of school and never stopped until the last.

"Whoa, Timminy, hope I didn't step on you. Didn't see you down there."

"Eeny-meeny-MINNY-mo. No shorties on our team, no, no, no!"

"Phew—I'm tired. Mind if I rest my elbow on your head?"

Everyone was a clown.

If only it weren't a *new* school. At my last school, I'd found a group of "safe" kids to hang with. We were all different in our own ways—allergic to every food on the planet, streak of white hair, missing-three-fingers birth defect, stutter, glasses thicker than hockey pucks, and me the shorty. We weren't best buds, but we got along and had a silent agreement to never make an issue of one another's issues. Maybe Skenago Middle School would have its own misfits club I could join.

If only it weren't a *middle* school. I was supposed to be a fifth grader, the oldest grade at my old elementary school. Fifth graders were the kings and queens there. I'd have been happy to be a short emperor like Napoleon. But instead, fifth grade was the *baby* grade at Skenago Middle School.

But most of all . . . if only it weren't *Dad's* school. As the assistant principal, he'd see how much I was teased. He'd been a father a lot longer than he'd been an assistant principal, and there's no way his dad instincts wouldn't kick in. The thought of being rescued by my dad in front of the other kids made me cringe and shrink. And the last thing I needed was to shrink any more.

I started tossing and turning again. The sheet felt like a ghost choking me. How was it possible to have a nightmare when I wasn't even asleep?

Just then, Maxi pushed my door open with her snout. She was checking on me, like she did every night, right after she checked on Mom and Dad and before she settled down in the hallway between our two bedrooms where she could guard both rooms all night long.

"Help me, girl," I whispered when she sniffed up over the edge of the mattress.

She couldn't hear me even if I'd shouted, so I whispered again, "I mean it—help me. Please." Maxi put her front paws on the mattress and looked at me. The full moon glowed through the skylight directly above my bed.

Maxi stared at me, deep, past my eyes, to the inside.

"I need you," I whispered, or maybe I only thought it.

Maxi never took her eyes from mine as she backed up, then leaped forward onto my bed for the first time by herself. She nudged the twisted covers and somehow released them, freeing me from being a bed mummy. Then she pressed her head into my chest, giving me a Maxi hug.

"Thank you, girl. I needed that."

Her head tilted and she lapped my face. Then she curled up next to me and laid her head on my chest, pushing down ever so gently, every few seconds, gently, slowly, slowly, gently—changing my breaths from short pants to calming sighs.

"Maybe, just maybe I can do this, girl. If you say so."

SECRET #8

It's possible to hear someone even if your ears don't work.

CHAPTER 9

THE NEXT MORNING, I gave Maxi a big hug and said, "Enjoy your last bit of freedom, girl, before Mom leaves for work and shuts you in your crate for the rest of the day. I promise I'll get back as fast as I can after school so we can play."

Dad and I were quiet the whole ride into school.

"Glad you rode with me, Timminy. It's a big day for both of us. Want a tour?" Dad asked as we pulled into the parking lot.

"Nah, thanks, Dad. I have my schedule, so I'll check things out and then find you in your office. It won't take long. There's not even a second floor. That's great. Us short kids like short schools."

"'We.' It's 'we,'" said Dad.

I clenched my jaw. "Got it, Mr. Once-an-English-Teacher-Always-an-English-Teacher. You're right. Wee-wee—that's ME!"

"I meant the pronoun, Timminy. Not your size. Calm down and give this school a chance."

"Only if it gives *me* a chance." I stomped off. Dad was smart enough not to stop me.

I found each of my rooms. There were only three—a homeroom, and then one class for all the language arts and history stuff, and another for math and science. Then I scouted out the art room, library, gym, and cafeteria.

There were stools at one table in the art room. Good, that would make me look taller. The cafeteria had a table in a corner close to the door, near both the serving line and return-tray drop-off—a perfect place to sit where I wouldn't have to do any long grand entrances or exits and have all eyes staring at the new *short* kid.

I heard doors closing and talking down a hallway so I hurried down another hallway to the front of the school, saw an ASSISTANT PRINCIPAL plaque over a doorway, and slipped into Dad's office. He wasn't there. I was glad. It was still early and school didn't start until 7:50. I could hide here until it was time to go to homeroom.

I noticed Dad had family photos in his office. Ugh! How was I supposed to remain anonymous? I shifted the photos around, hiding them behind books and putting a solo one of Maxi front and center. Maxi would be a good distraction—"Aww, what a cute puppy."

There was a knock at the door. I froze, hoping whoever it was would go away. They didn't. The door

opened. "Hello, hello . . . Mr. Harris, are you there?"
The door opened wider.

"Sorry, I was looking for Mr. Harris. Do you know where he is?"

"Nope."

"Are you supposed to be in his office? All alone?"

"Yup."

"Wait a minute, are you Timminy Harris?"

Now I was stuck. I wanted to say nope again to make this woman go away, but she *did* pronounce my name correctly. No one ever pronounced my name correctly.

I shrugged.

She held out her hand. "Nice to meet you, Timminy. You're the reason I stopped by. I wanted to ask your dad where you were so I could meet you before the day started. I'm Ms. Sanborn, your homeroom teacher. See you in a little while."

That was it. She left as fast as she came. No fanfare. No odd looks or comments. Maybe this school wouldn't be *all* bad.

BANG!

The door burst back open.

Someone was yelling.

"IF YOU'RE SENDING ME TO THE ASSISTANT PRINCIPAL'S OFFICE, I'M *NOT* WAITING OUT HERE. LET'S GET THIS OVER WITH."

"But I told you Mr. Harris isn't in his office right

now. You'll have to wait outside, Rory." The woman I figured was the secretary was trying to sound stern, but I could tell she was a teddy-bear type.

I saw who it was—the Jerk.

Then he saw me.

"Hey, it's you, shrimp. Whatcha doing in the AP's office? I'm always the first one sent to the AP's. You trying to ruin my reputation or what? Get outta here."

"No problem, Roar-y," I said as I stepped around him. It was pronounced the same so the Jerk didn't know I was calling him Roary instead of Rory, but I liked my little joke. I smirked and stepped out of the office right into Dad's chest.

"What's going on in here?" he asked, looking from the Jerk to me and back again.

"Nothing, Dad. I'm just leaving. Roary here is your first customer of the year."

Dad raised his eyebrows. "Not so fast, Timminy. Wait for me out here."

The door closed behind him. I sat down and strained to listen to what kind of trouble the Jerk had gotten himself into before the first day of school had even started. At the same time, I tried to hide behind a magazine I'd picked up, hoping no one would see me waiting outside the assistant principal's office. I couldn't hear a thing. They must make administrators' doors extra thick to protect students' privacy. But what about my dad's

39

safety? The Jerk could have my dad in a headlock and no one would be able to hear his screams for help. I leaned closer, but I may as well have been as deaf as Maxi sitting there.

Click—the door opened. I scurried to sit back in my chair and look nonchalant, peeking over the magazine.

"Yes, sir, Mr. Harris, I understand. There's no need to call my dad. There won't be any more trouble on the bus," Rory said as he left Dad's office.

What was this? Did my dad have assistant-principal superpowers already? He'd tamed the Jerk.

As he passed me, Rory whispered, "So you're the new AP's son? Living right next door to me. I'll see you around the neighborhood, shrimp. Oh, wait, what'd your dad call you—Minny? Perfect name for you and easy to remember. Enjoy the pictures in your magazine, Minny."

He left with a smile and nod as he walked past my dad. I looked down and saw the magazine I'd picked up. *Humpty Dumpty*! Why'd they have *Humpty Dumpty* in a middle school? Then I realized they must be for little brothers and sisters who had to come to school with their parents whenever their big brothers and sisters got into trouble.

The bell rang. I stood up to leave, and Dad stopped me.

"Timminy."

"Yes, Dad?"

"Remember, it's probably best to call me Mr. Harris at school. Now get going. You don't want to be late for homeroom the first day."

I stepped into the hallway, looked with longing at the front door, and wondered whether I'd get into trouble if I skipped school . . .

For the whole year.

SECRET #9
Staying home and sleeping in a crate isn't the worst way to spend a day.

CHAPTER 10

I'D ONLY TAKEN a few steps into the hallway of my new school when a tall, athletic girl stopped me. Was *every* kid in this school a giant? She leaned down and asked, "May I help you?"

I kept walking.

She followed me. "I'm on the student council. Probably I'll be elected president this year—you can trust me."

I still kept walking.

Her legs were so long she took one step to three of mine. This time she stepped in front and cut me off.

"Please let me help you," she insisted.

I sighed. "I'm fine. It's my first day here."

"Yes, but I think you're at the wrong school. The bus stops here at the middle school first and then goes to the elementary school. You just got off the bus too soon. Come with me. I'll take you to the office and get this straightened out."

Then she patted me on the head, like I was a dog or something. If only I could bite her hand to make her stop.

Instead I swallowed so hard I made a gargling, not a growling sound, and said, "I go to school *here*. I'm new. In fifth grade."

Student-council girl gasped. "Really?"

I nodded.

She gasped again. "I'm so sorry. I was trying to help. I really thought you were at the wrong school—by mistake. My mistake. Sorry, sorry, sor . . ."

Then she raced away with those long legs. Probably worried she'd lost my vote.

She was right—she had.

As I walked toward homeroom, a group of boys jammed the hallway. There was no way to walk around them, only through them. So I put my head down and tried to find the quickest way through without being noticed.

I flunked!

"Look, guys, a new one."

"Yeah, a real pipsqueak."

"Hey, shrimpy, where you from?"

I lowered my head even more, said, "Excuse me," and tried again to make my way through without touching any of them.

But one of them touched me. Put a finger to my chest

and said, "Hey, shorty, we're talking to YOU. Where you from?"

I still kept my eyes down. Sort of like not looking a vicious dog in the eyes—to try to avoid an attack. (Not that I knew anything about vicious dogs. Maxi was the opposite of vicious. She loved everyone—probably even these losers.)

"Portland," I answered.

"Oh, from the big city. That explains your mucky-muck attitude. Out here in the sticks, we answer when people—"

Someone interrupted. "Hey, guys. Isn't the new assistant principal from Portland?"

Finger boy stabbed me in the chest again. "What's your last name? Harris?"

I gulped, saw a gap between two of the boys, and quickly darted through.

"Hey, get back here, squirt."

"Who do you think you are?"

"We're not done talking to you."

I heard big footsteps behind me. I could see the headline in the newspaper: TINY MIDDLE SCHOOLER SQUISHED DEAD LIKE A BUG ON FIRST DAY OF SCHOOL. I ran down the hall. Good thing I'd scouted out my classrooms before school. I raced past a few more doors and burst into homeroom, trying to catch my breath and act cool all at the same time.

Ms. Sanborn nodded at me. "Everything okay, Timminy?"

I nodded back, put on a fake smile, and decided against telling her about my recent male bonding experience.

Ms. Sanborn smiled a real smile and said, "You're just in time. We're all heading back out to the hall."

"Hall?" I gulped.

"Yes." She handed me a paper. "Here's your locker assignment and combination."

I didn't look at it. The only combination I could imagine was a deadly one: 1 Shrimp + 1 Mob of Angry Boys = 1 Less Shrimp in the World.

I stalled and headed to the back of the line, hoping the angry boys would be gone by the time I got out there.

I peeked both ways, didn't see any of them—although I had no idea what they looked like. During our "chat," all I saw was their big feet.

"Right here, Timminy." Ms. Sanborn pointed at locker 168. "Why don't you practice your combination a few times? Did you have lockers at your school in Portland? Here at Skenago Middle School, lockers are the bane of many a fifth grader's existence."

Bane of existence? What the heck did that mean? This Ms. Sanborn sounded like my dad, throwing around fancy-schmancy words.

I focused on the lock . . . 22 right, 18 left, 9 right . . . nothing happened.

Again—22 right, 18 left, 9 right . . . still nothing.

"Want some help?" The beaming boy at the locker to my right was practically busting out of his shirt, all ready to give tours of his *open* locker.

"No, thanks."

22 right, 18 left, 9 right . . . NOTHING!

"Oh, let me try it." He grabbed the paper from my hand and started spinning the lock . . . 22 right, 18 left, 9 right . . . OPEN!

"See. I've got the magic touch," he said.

"Then maybe you can make yourself disappear," I mumbled.

I wished magic-touch boy and angry boys and student-council girl would *all* disappear. They were all the bane of my existence—whatever that meant.

SECRET #10

When all you want is to be left alone, that's exactly when the world swarms you like a mob of thirsty mosquitoes.

CHAPTER 11

MOST KIDS COMPLAIN about their classes and say things like:

"Adverbs are the enemy."

"Who cares what dead people did two hundred years ago?"

"All I need to know about black holes is that my brain is one!"

I don't get it though. Classes are the *safe* part of school.

I hate the in-between parts—before school, break time, passing between classes, lunch. All potential land mines that can blow up any second. And when you're closer to the ground, land mines are more dangerous, much more dangerous.

My next potential land mine—lunch!

I'd brought in lunch so I wouldn't have to stand in the lunch line the first day—on display for the whole cafeteria to see. Plus who knew what they served in Ske-nago. Probably squirrel stew or moose mousse or something else made from what they shot in the woods. My lunch in hand, all I needed was an out-of-the-way place to sit and eat. I headed toward the corner table I'd scoped out before school, but . . .

It was already filled with laughing, chitchatting kids. *Popular* kids.

I put my head down and headed toward the back of the cafeteria, using my peripheral vision to look for an empty table. But I admit a tiny part of me dared to hope for more—that someone from one of my morning classes would flag me down and say, "Hey, aren't you the new kid in our math class? Don't be so obtuse. Come sit with us." Math geeks—yup, I'd be happy eating with math geeks.

No invitations.

And no empty tables.

Finally, I spotted an almost-empty table with two guys who had their noses stuck in books, and I grabbed a seat. The only book I had with me was my math book, so I flipped it open and started reading the chapter assigned for tomorrow.

But I couldn't concentrate. Our table was so quiet, pieces of conversations from other tables floated by . . . "that him?" . . . "such a squirt" . . . "from Portland" . . .

and laughter. Lots of laughter from every direction. Were they laughing at *me*? I didn't dare to look. But I could feel their stares like X-ray vision cutting right through me.

"So short" . . . "Daddy's boy" . . . "Tiny Tim" . . .

Did someone really say Tiny Tim? Did kids already know who I was? I'd always heard there was no keeping secrets from middle schoolers.

Since they were onto me, I wondered whether I should escape from lunch early or wait until the last possible second to avoid them all. Leaving early meant hanging in the hall where the angry boys hung out, so I decided to stay late. Almost everyone was gone when the bell rang and now I had to hurry to history class.

But as I left the cafeteria . . .

"HEY, MINNY! HEY, KEVIN!"

The Jerk. Of course, the Jerk. The *last* person I wanted to see.

But who was Kevin? I looked behind me and *gulp*! There was another bruiser—almost as big as Rory. Man, what do they put in the water up here in Skenago? Whatever it is, I'd better start drinking it—gallons of it.

"Wanna join me for lunch, guys?" asked Rory.

BURRRRRRRP! Kevin belched so loud I swear the cafeteria floor shook as if he'd triggered an earthquake.

Rory fist-bumped Kevin to congratulate him on his

burp and said, "Oh yeah, I forgot you still have the early lunch this year."

"I already ate too," I said.

"That's right," Rory snorted. "You eat with the *little* kids."

I felt steam coming out of my ears, like an angry cartoon character. I stretched my neck as tall as it would go—to get right in the Jerk's face (I made it to his lowest rib) and said, "At least *I* didn't get sent to the office before the first day of school even started." I felt like adding, "Take *that*!" But Rory snorted again and high-fived that Kevin guy. He wasn't embarrassed about being sent to Dad's office—he was proud of it.

Then Kevin let out another ground-shaking burp and smiled.

"Get a bib," I suggested before stomping away.

I went to history class, but really only my body went. My mind was already home, with Maxi. That's how I was going to make it through the day. I kept telling myself, "Can't wait to see you, girl. Can't wait to see you, girl. Can't wait . . ." It didn't matter that Maxi couldn't hear me. It only mattered that *I* could hear it. I kept my Maxi message playing in my head the rest of the day until Mom picked me up after school and brought me home.

Seems Maxi couldn't wait to see me either. When I let

her out of her crate, she went crazy. She jumped up, knocked me to the floor, and smothered me with kisses — all over, sticking her tongue up my nostrils, in my ears. She even licked inside my belly button. It was like she was trying to kiss me on the inside, where I needed it the most.

SECRET #11
There's nothing so bad in the world that dog kisses won't make it better.

CHAPTER 12

WAS IT TOO LATE to add an extra class—How to Open a Locker for Dummies?

22 right, 18 left, 9 right . . . nothing.

22 right, 18 left, 9 right . . . *still* nothing!

The second day of school wasn't going to be any better than the first.

22 right, 18 left, 9 right . . . *click*—OPEN!

Maybe it would be better after all. I looked right to see if magic-touch boy was watching me. He wasn't, but I lingered with the door open in case he or anyone else walked by and wanted to admire my nimble-finger locker success.

BUMP!

BANG!

"DANG!" Maybe I was better off *not* opening my locker! Now I'd been shoved *inside* it. But before I could figure a way out, I heard a commotion . . .

"Let him out."

"Pick on somebody your own size, you big oaf."

"Anybody know the combination?"

I heard jostling and jimmying and spinning and . . . OPEN!

There stood magic-touch boy. "You're welcome. Don't worry—now I'll make myself disappear." He walked off. Can't say I blamed him.

The Jerk wasn't anywhere in sight now, but I knew he was to blame. That chicken ran off, but wait till I had a chance to get even. I'd . . . I'd . . . bite him in the ankles!

"Are you all right?" Someone from behind patted me on the head.

Not again! I turned. It was student-council girl.

"I'm fine."

"You sure?" She leaned down in my face.

"Yes."

"Don't worry," she said. "We'll report this."

Her friends all nodded.

"Please don't. I'm okay. It's no big deal."

"Yes, it is a big deal. We strive to make our school safe for everyone."

I fake smiled again. I knew what she meant. Everyone = shrimp like me. The only thing worse than getting shoved into a locker because I'm so small I fit was getting let out of a locker because I'm so small everyone pitied me. There's nothing worse than being the guest of honor at a pity party.

Student-council girl and her friends stood in a semicircle around me with their best pouty, sympathetic looks. I stepped away before they *all* started patting me on the head.

"Don't worry. I'm okay. And please *don't* report this. You see, I . . . I . . . I was actually giving that big oaf a hard time before he shoved me into my locker. I had it coming."

"Really?" Student-council girl looked skeptical.

"Yup, I know I wasn't playing fair—that you should pick on someone your *own* size." Then I winked.

Everyone burst out laughing.

Just what I was hoping for. "See you around," I said as I started to walk off.

"Wait. What's your name?" asked student-council girl.

"Timminy."

"See you around, Timminy."

"And your name?" I asked.

"Kassy, with a *K*."

"'Kay, Kassy with a *K*, see you around."

Then Kassy with a *K* winked at *me*!

Maybe she still had a chance to earn my vote for prez—if only she'd stop patting me.

When I went into homeroom, I said thanks to magic-touch boy.

Then Ms. Sanborn made me stay after the bell rang for first period.

"Timminy, since you come to school so early with your dad—"

"With Mr. Harris," I said.

"Yes, Mr. Harris." She grinned. "Feel free to come into homeroom early. You can do your homework, but fair warning . . . I might ask you to help me with some of my work too."

"'Kay. Thanks," I said as I smiled a *real* smile. I wasn't sure if Ms. Sanborn had seen the whole shut-in-my-locker fiasco. But even if she did, I had to give her credit for not mentioning it, for giving me the best pass—a chance to avoid one of the in-between parts of school. Would I go to her homeroom early? Heck, yeah! Even if she offered 'cause she pitied me? Oh, heck, yeah!

SECRET #12
The combination to unlock middle school survival is one big mystery.

CHAPTER 13

SOMEHOW I SURVIVED the first week of school—
which was only three whole days. (Maybe starting school
the Wednesday before Labor Day wasn't such a bad idea
after all!)

And I didn't spend any more time inside lockers—
thanks to Ms. Sanborn letting me kill time in her room
before school.

I *did* get passed like a hot potato between those big
boys in the hall after school on Friday, but they all put
on their innocent faces and disappeared when my dad
stepped around the corner.

Dad looked suspicious and asked, "You okay,
Timminy?"

"I'm great, Mr. Harris."

And I *was* great—now that it was finally the long
weekend and it was going to be all Maxi all the time!

My plan for Labor Day weekend was *no* plans. Mom and Dad agreed since they were tired after their first week of working with kids. Plus it was supposed to be blistering hot for late summer. Doing nothing in the house with the AC blasting sounded perfect. Maxi and I could watch movies and play computer games.

But my no-plans plan changed when the FedEx truck backed up the driveway Saturday morning. I'd taken Maxi out to do her business, but she'd gotten distracted by a stick.

Beep-beep-beep!

"Stop! Stop!" I yelled, trying to catch the driver's eye in his side or rearview mirror. I stepped in back of his truck, waved my arms wildly, and hollered louder, "STOP!"

He *did* stop and jumped out with his face all in a pucker. "Hey, kid, you're too short to step behind a truck that's backing up. I almost didn't see you. Are you crazy?"

I puckered up my own face and pointed at Maxi lying in the driveway behind me. "If you couldn't see me, then did you see *her*?"

The driver answered. "No, but she would have moved with my back-up signal."

"No, she wouldn't. She's deaf."

"Really? A deaf puppy?"

"Yup."

"Sorry. I didn't know. I've always backed up to this house from the turnaround spot in the driveway, but I won't do that any—"

Before the driver could finish, Maxi saw him, ran over, and jumped up on him with her front paws.

"Down, Maxi, down," I said.

The driver laughed. "She can't hear you. Remember? I don't mind. I love dogs."

Then he held his palm up in front of her face as a signal to stay. She *did*! He got in his truck and came out with a package in one hand and his other hand closed in a fist.

"Lynda Harris live here?" he asked.

"Yup, that's my mom."

"This is for her." He passed me the package.

Then he looked down at Maxi, who was staring at his closed hand. "And this is for you." He waved his fist in front of Maxi's nose. "Sit!" he commanded while pushing down on her butt with his other hand. He paused and when she held the sit position for a second, he opened his hand to give her the doggie treat. "Good dog."

"Thanks, mister," I said. For the first time, I realized that just because Maxi was deaf, it didn't mean she couldn't learn to follow directions.

"Now stand back, you two. I don't need any more close calls. And I promise to keep an eye out for this precious pup the next time I have a package to deliver."

"Thanks again," I said, holding Maxi back by her collar.

As he turned toward his truck, he said, "What are the odds? Deaf here and blind next door."

"Really?" I asked.

"Really," he said. "See you around."

He jumped into his truck and drove off.

I leaned down and kissed Maxi on her snout. "Maybe it's time we go meet our neighbors, girl."

SECRET #13
Sometimes when you least expect it, hope wiggles into your heart.

CHAPTER 14

I RACED INSIDE to let Dad know Maxi and I were going for a walk. "We'll be back soon," I hollered.

Dad stood at the bottom of the cellar stairs with his hands on his hips. "I thought you were going to help me unpack these last few boxes. Then we're free to take the rest of the weekend off."

"I will when I get back, Dad. It's just Maxi's been cooped up in her crate so much this week with school starting. I think she needs some exercise."

"All right. Where are you going?"

"Not far. We'll stay in the neighborhood."

"Hang on tight to her. Cars drive pretty fast along these rural roads. You'll have to be her ears."

"I've already figured that out, Dad. Be back soon."

All the houses in our neighborhood were set back from the road with long driveways and lots of property. As

Dad said, one reason to live out in the country is *not* to see your neighbors. What a change from Portland!

I certainly did *not* want to see Rory the Jerk. I didn't know which house was his, but it probably was nearby. I also didn't know which neighbor the FedEx driver was talking about when he said "blind next door." I wasn't sure why I was so excited about having a blind dog next door. Maybe because we wouldn't be the *only* ones in the neighborhood who were different.

We headed left at the bottom of our driveway and started up the next driveway. I walked beside Maxi with one hand on her leash and the other on her back to keep her calm if we saw the other dog.

Suddenly I heard shouting.

"I'LL BE BACK, DAD. GONNA SEE WHAT I SHOT."

Oh no! I recognized that voice. The Jerk! I heard his four-wheeler start up.

"Come on, Maxi. Let's get outta here before he shoots *us*!" It sounded like Rory was heading into the woods, not toward the road. But I couldn't be sure, so I ran back toward our driveway. The blind dog must be our neighbor on the other side. And now at least we knew where the Jerk lived. Too close!

The next driveway led us up a big hill to a gray house with red shutters and a white picket fence boxing in one side of the yard. No one was out front, so we made our way to the side. A fence was a perfect way to keep a blind dog safe. Heck, maybe we should get one to keep our deaf dog safe.

I peered over the fence and Maxi started sniffing between the slats.

First, I saw a pool. A *pool*! This was one neighbor I wanted to get friendly with fast! Like before-the-end-of-this-hot-weekend fast!

Then I saw a girl in a lounge chair.

But I didn't see a dog anywhere.

Woof! Woof! Suddenly Maxi barked.

"Who's there?" yelled the girl.

"It's me, your new neighbor, and my dog, Maxi."

"Oh, I heard someone had moved into the Gillespies' house. So your dog has a name. Do you?"

"Yes, I'm Timminy."

"Hi, I'm Abby. Come on in. The gate's on the back side of the fence."

"Thanks." I tugged Maxi toward the gate, stepped inside, and walked up behind her lounge chair. I kept talking. "Abby, you're not going to believe this. Maxi is deaf. What are the odds? My dog is *deaf* and your dog is *blind*. How funny is that?"

As I stepped in front of Abby, I almost tripped on the cane leaning against her chair. And then I saw *her* eyes— smaller, sunken, different.

"Oh my gosh! I'm so sorry."

"For what?" asked Abby.

"*You're* blind. I'm sorry. I didn't know."

"It's not your fault. I was born blind."

"I know it's not my fault *you're* blind. But it's my fault I assumed your *dog* was blind."

"I don't have a dog," said Abby. "And if I did, I don't think a blind dog would be a good match for me."

"No, of course not," I kept blubbering. "The blind shouldn't lead the blind. Oh crap! That's not what I meant to say. What I meant is . . . No, no, NO, MAXI!"

Maxi's leash had slipped out of my hand and now she had her paws up on Abby's shoulders.

"Down, Maxi, down! Oh no, I'm sorry. Down, down, down!"

"Shush up!" said Abby. "And don't move."

I froze and held my breath as Maxi sniffed at Abby's eyes. Then Abby closed them and Maxi gently licked each eye, one after the other.

Abby smiled. "Maxi? Is that a girl or a boy name?"

I wasn't sure if I was still under shush-up orders, but I said, "It's short for Maxine. My dad named her. I saved her with the nickname Maxi. And Timminy is a boy name."

"I figured that out. I'm blind, not stupid," Abby said.

"Sorry."

"Oooooh! If you say sorry, one more time, I'm kicking you out."

"Sorry."

"That's it!" yelled Abby. "Get out of here, but Maxi can stay."

On cue, Maxi lay down next to Abby's chair and nudged her hand to make sure she got some pats.

"Fine," I said and turned to go. Then stopped. "Are you crazy? I'm not leaving Maxi here. She's the one who sniffed and lapped your eyes. You should be mad at *her*. Not me."

Abby laughed. "That's better. You can stay." She gestured toward the empty lounge chair beside her.

"No. I'll go. Come on, Maxi." I tugged on her collar, but she didn't move.

Abby laughed harder.

I took the bait. "What's so funny?"

"You keep talking to Maxi and she can't hear you."

"I forget. We found out last week, so I'm still getting used to it. But I think I'll always talk to her. That's one of the reasons to have a dog, for the company."

"Wish I had a dog."

I finally sat down. "I thought blind people got Seeing Eye dogs."

Abby sighed. "Blind grown-ups can get guide dogs— that's what we call them—but not kids. I'm stuck with this cane. It's not the best company," she said. "You have to be sixteen to get a dog. I have almost four more years to wait, actually three years, seven months, and fourteen days, but who's counting?"

"That's not fair," I said.

"Tell me about not fair," said Abby.

All I could see were her eyes again and I couldn't help it, I said, "Sorry." 'Cause I was.

"There you go again. Cut it out. If you're gonna feel sorry for me, you can move back to wherever you came from."

"Portland," I said.

"Good, that's far enough away so you won't bug me. I don't need your sympathy. I find that everywhere I go. I know everyone stares at me. I hear their whispers, 'She's blind. Poor girl. How awful.'"

"That stinks," I said. When she didn't say anything, I added, "But not as much as Maxi stinks!"

When Abby asked, "What do you mean?" I told her about Maxi's car ride home from the breeder's. Abby laughed and laughed as she kept patting Maxi. I exaggerated only a little—nothing like a good old poop story to clear the air.

"Lunchtime, Abby!" A woman stepped out from the house onto the patio. "Oh, you have guests."

"It's the new neighbors, Mom. Timminy and his dog, Maxi."

"Nice to meet you, Abby's mom." I stood and nodded.

"Kate Winslow—just call me Kate. Want to stay for lunch? I probably can find another can of SpaghettiOs to open."

I waited for her to laugh or wink or something. When she didn't, I said, "Er, no thanks. And if you don't mind, I'll call you Mrs. Winslow." (If Dad made me call *him* Mr. Harris at school, I didn't think he'd want me calling her by her first name.) I continued, "Maxi and I need to head home. I promised my dad we wouldn't be gone long."

On cue, Maxi stood up (how'd she keep doing that if she was deaf?), ambled over to Mrs. Winslow, and held her head up for some puppy loving. Mrs. Winslow obliged. "Sweet pup. Wish we had a dog, or better yet a whole sled full of dogs to get around in these Maine winters."

"Mom, we live in Maine, not Alaska."

Mrs. Winslow shrugged her shoulders. "Not much difference," she said. "Gotta stir the SpaghettiOs before they burn. Don't be long, Abby. Nice meeting you, Timothy."

"Timminy," I corrected her. "It's a special family name."

"Lucky you. We're . . ." She paused and smiled. "A special family." Then she stepped inside.

I stood there with my mouth open, then said, "Your mom is . . ."

"A comedian?" asked Abby. "She thinks she is. Dad and I don't encourage her by laughing. You shouldn't either."

"Yeah, that, but I was thinking more that she's wh—"

"White? How observant, Timminy. So's my dad. I'm adopted. But I give you credit that you only seemed shocked I was blind, not black, earlier. That's pretty good considering we live in the whitest state in the country."

"At my old school in Portland, we had lots of black students, many immigrant families from Somalia and Sudan. They didn't always speak English and had accents. You don't have any accent."

"Ayuh! A Maine one." Abby smirked. "Maybe because I was born in Chicago, but I've been a Maine-uh since I was four months old. Gotta go in for lunch." She stood up.

"Need some help?" I asked.

"Nah! I have every square inch of our house and yard memorized—unless something is out of place. But then this cane will let me know."

Suddenly she turned right, not left.

Toward the pool, not the house.

Without using her cane.

She took four steps toward the pool and lifted her right foot over the water. I shouted, "ABBY!"

"Gotcha!" Abby laughed as she pulled her foot back.

"How could I ever have felt sorry for you?" I said.

"Glad to see your mom isn't the only comedian in the family."

Abby smiled proudly and walked back toward their patio, using her cane this time. When she touched Maxi—Maxi who was peeking through the glass doors, probably hoping to try her first SpaghettiOs—she leaned down and ran her fingers through Maxi's fur. Her smile grew bigger as she said, "Hey, girl, you must be hot with all that fur. Why don't you come back over after lunch and cool off with a doggie paddle in the pool?"

Maxi barked one of her happy barks.

"Are you sure your dog is deaf?" asked Abby.

"So they tell me."

She picked up the end of Maxi's leash and tossed it right to me.

"Are you sure you're blind?" I asked.

"So they tell me," said Abby.

I tugged on Maxi's leash and headed toward the back gate.

As Abby headed inside, she turned and said, "Maxi, if you want to bring that silly boy of yours over with you for a swim after lunch, we'll try to put up with him."

SECRET #14
Sometimes you shouldn't be so sure of what you think you're sure of.

CHAPTER 15

MOM AND DAD thought it was a great idea that Maxi and I were going to Abby's for a swim after lunch. It turned out Dad had already met Abby and her parents at a meeting at school.

"Does Abby go to our school?" I asked. "I haven't seen her."

"Why don't you ask Abby that?" he said.

I did as soon as we went back over.

"Yup, I've always gone to Skenago schools," she said. "I'm in sixth grade. I'll be starting this coming week, since my new ed tech was finishing up her training last week."

"Ed tech?" I asked.

"Teacher aide. I have my own teacher aide to help me at school."

"That's good."

"Not always," said Abby. "Maybe good for the

schoolwork, but it stinks for my social life. Who wants to talk to someone who has a grown-up hanging around all the time? But if I had a guide dog instead, I bet everyone would want to hang out with me."

"Well, I'm only in fifth grade, but maybe we could hang out at school."

"Sure. We'll share the same lunch period."

"Then I'll look for you," I said.

"And I'll *listen* for you," Abby said.

My laugh was interrupted by a . . .

SPLASH!

Maxi had jumped into the pool! The deep end!

"Maxi! No, Maxi!" I dove in after her, sneakers and all.

Abby sat in her chair laughing.

"It's not funny," I yelled as I reached for Maxi. "She's never been in the water before."

"Calm down, Timminy. She'll be fine. Sounds like she's doing the doggie paddle."

I stopped flailing my arms and just treaded water. Abby was right. Maxi was swimming. "Good, girl."

"You sound like a proud parent."

I smiled. "Guess I am."

Now that I knew Maxi had things under control, I climbed out, ditched my sneakers and the clothes I'd had on over my bathing suit, and jumped back in with Maxi. Abby joined us too.

After a while, Abby's mom brought out a pitcher of

lemonade for us and a bowl of water for Maxi. Maxi beat us out of the pool, walking up the steps on the shallow end. She slurped from the water dish, then shook off right next to Mrs. Winslow.

"Just what I needed, Maxi," Mrs. Winslow said, laughing. "A cold shower on this hot day."

"And I need some of that cold lemonade, Mom," said Abby.

"Help yourself," said Mrs. Winslow. "My waitress days are over."

Abby laughed. "Then I'll be your waitress."

I tried not to stare, but I couldn't help myself as I watched Abby pour lemonade for each of us. She put a little contraption with metal prongs over the side of the glass. It made a high-pitched noise when the lemonade touched the prongs. She didn't spill a drop.

"That's so cool, Abby," I said.

"It's called a liquid indicator," she said. "Good thing I'm only blind and not deaf too so I can hear it beep."

When Abby said "deaf," I turned to look at Maxi, but she had . . . disappeared.

"Uh-oh! Where's Maxi?" I said.

Mrs. Winslow looked all around.

Abby asked, "Is the gate open, or the door to the house?"

"No," I said as my eyes darted from one to the other.

I jumped up and checked the pool. Phew! That was

empty. The fence was too tall—Maxi couldn't have jumped it. I checked the bottom of the fence to see if she'd dug *under* it.

Mrs. Winslow started laughing and pointed.

I laughed too, relieved.

Abby groaned. "It's times like these I hate being blind. You both found her and it's funny and I can't see the joke."

"Sorry," I said.

"What'd I tell you about 'sorry,'" said Abby. "I don't need 'sorry.' I need to get the joke."

Mrs. Winslow started, "Imagine—"

"Mom," Abby interrupted, "let Timminy try. If he's going to be my friend, he needs to learn *blind talk*."

"Blind talk?" I asked.

"Yes, you have to tell me what's so funny about where you found Maxi, but you can't use 'seeing' words."

"That sounds hard," I said.

"Give it a try," Abby said.

"Um, Maxi, my big, white Great Pyrenees puppy is peeking out of the big green shade plants growing next to your garage. She looks like a white ghost peeking out of a green jungle." I smiled proudly. "How's that? Pretty good for my first *blind talk*, huh?"

"Gong!" said Abby.

"You failed," said Mrs. Winslow.

"What do you mean? I thought I did a good job describing things."

Abby sighed. "You used 'seeing' words. Big—I can't see big. White and green—I can't see colors."

Her mom added, "A big, furry dog peeking out from the plants as she tries to cool down . . . Abby knows what those words mean, but she can't feel the joke. You have to use hearing or taste or touch or smell words so Abby can understand in a way that makes sense to her senses."

"How do I do that?"

Mrs. Winslow said, "You could say something like Maxi is a loud, screeching note of rock music in the middle of a soft symphony."

Abby grinned. "That's pretty good, Mom. See, Timminy, that lets me know how out of place, what a surprise Maxi was when you saw her. You try."

"Hmmm, let me think . . ."

Abby waited, Mrs. Winslow waited, and Maxi didn't care as she slept in the shade.

I gave it another try. "Maxi is hiding like . . . a . . . a marshmallow in the middle of a big bowl of broccoli."

Abby laughed. "Not bad. You might get this blind talk with practice."

I smiled. "Practice" meant I'd get to see Abby again.

SECRET #15

A new friend is like a wrapped present—you're not sure what's inside, but you can't wait to find out.

CHAPTER 16

I SAW ABBY again on Monday when we met the Winslows in front of the fudge shop on Main Street for the Skenago Labor Day parade.

When they walked up, I noticed Abby didn't have her cane and was holding on to her dad's arm instead.

"Forget your cane?" I asked.

"No, parades are too busy," answered Abby. "My cane would be tapping something in every direction—system overload. And I might trip someone."

"And how come you're wearing dark glasses today?"

"I wear them in public so I don't upset people when they see my eyes. Remember your reaction to my eyes?"

"I was just surprised, that's all."

"Yeah, right. Tell me about it, Timminy. I was there, remember?"

"Yeah, I remember."

"Someday, I hope I'll be confident enough not to

wear dark glasses in public. And if my eyes bother people, it'll be their problem, not mine."

"I like your attitude, Abby Winslow," I said.

"I will too if I'm ever that brave—not there yet."

Woo-Woo-Woo! A police siren blared as the parade kicked off.

My mom said, "Ooh, it's starting. I love parades. How great that Skenago has a Labor Day parade. Portland never did."

Abby's dad nodded. "Skenago has a parade for every holiday—Halloween, Fourth of July, Flag Day, Thanksgiving, Groundhog Day. But you'd better bundle up for the New Year's Eve midnight parade. It gets pretty cold. Small towns don't need a reason to celebrate—we just like getting together. And truth be told, our parades pretty much all look alike. Abby and I mostly come because we're fudge fans."

I turned to Abby. "So it's all about the fudge?"

Abby grinned. "And the sounds too . . . the sirens, laughter, babies crying, drums drumming, flutes fluting, trumpets—"

I jumped in. "Trumpeting, oboes oboe-ing."

Abby laughed. "*Shhhhhh!* I don't want to miss a sound."

I watched Abby watch the parade, and closed my eyes several times to try to experience it the same way she did. *Clunk, hoot, cough, bang, bump, screech, snort, growl.* So many sounds. I felt a little dizzy.

Once when I opened my eyes to see what was making the *putt-putt-vroom* sounds right in front of us, I saw a group of clowns on scooters and one big clown on a four-wheeler.

The big clown drove closer—*vroom-vroom.* "Hey, Ab-B-B-B, I see you met Minny. You coming to school this week?" It was the Jerk.

Abby answered, "I met Timminy, if that's who you mean. And, yeah, I'll be in school tomorrow."

Rory nodded. "See you tomorrow, Ab-B-B-B. You too, Minny."

Ahooga-ahooga. A Model-A Ford signaled Rory to move along. Thank goodness!

The whole parade was over in a flash. It was the shortest one I'd ever seen, about twelve minutes tops. It took us longer to get our fudge.

Fudge Fantasy was mobbed, and there were soooo many choices. I settled on root beer float and Abby had blueberry cheesecake blast and we tasted each other's. "Yum," we said at the same time.

"When I turn sixteen, the first thing I'm going to do, after I get my guide dog, is get a job here," said Abby. "They won't have to pay me, just feed me fudge."

"You'll be a fudge blimp," I said. "And how are you going to give customers the right fudge if you can't see it?"

"I'll smell it. That's how."

"Nose prints on my fudge—SNOT nice."

Abby's arm shot out at me. I dodged, and she missed.

"Oooh, I owe you one."

"Since you can't see me, Abby, I want you to know I'm shaking in my shoes."

"Mom, Dad, let's go," Abby said. "I've had enough of this new neighbor of ours."

I could tell Abby was kidding. And I actually weaseled my way into riding back with Abby and her parents so I'd have a chance to talk with her. But instead, her dad gave us a play-by-play of the whole town, pointing out each business, plus who lived in each house, till we got to our neighborhood.

"Of course Rory Pelletier and his dad live up this driveway on the other side of your house," Mr. Winslow said. "Saw he was talking to you at the parade—so you must already know him."

"Not really," I said. "I've seen him around."

"I think he's in seventh grade this year. Right, Abby?"

"Yup," she answered.

I gulped. How could that giant Jerk *only* be in seventh grade? That meant Dad and I would have to put up with him in middle school another *whole* year!

"He's kinda big for a seventh grader," I said.

"Yeah, I think he stayed back a year," said Abby.

"Probably when his parents went through their divorce," added her dad. "I don't think Rory even sees his mom anymore. He has an older brother, Jeff, who dropped out of school and left town last year—not sure where he is. Rory's dad used to be a long-distance trucker and was away a lot. But when Jeff left, he changed jobs to drive a logging truck for the paper mill so he'd be home every night. He tries hard to do what's right for Rory."

I nodded as we pulled into Abby's driveway. If they didn't know Rory was a jerk, I wasn't going to be the one to break it to them. And they could stop with Rory's sob story—he's the last guy I'd throw a pity party for.

When we got to their house, I walked with them to the front door and said, "I gotta head home, give Maxi some attention, and finish my homework before tomorrow." Abby's parents said bye and headed inside. It was just the two of us.

"Um, before I go, Abby, I wanted to talk with you about something."

"When I'm planning to get revenge on you?"

"No, something serious."

"I didn't know you had a serious side. What's up?"

"Back at the parade, did you hear what Rory called me?"

"Minny, right? So he's already turned Timminy into a nickname. He must think you're special."

"Not so much." I looked away. Even though Abby couldn't see me, I still didn't want to face her. "The reason he called me Minny is because I'm . . ." I hesitated.

"Short?" asked Abby.

"Yes, how'd you know?"

Abby smiled. "Because I can tell the direction your voice comes from when you talk to me—down low, not from on high."

"Not funny, Abby. I'm short, really short, probably the shortest kid in school. Thought you should know in case you don't want to be seen with me at school."

"Stand still right in front of me," said Abby.

"Why?"

"So I can knock some sense into you." Abby reached out with her knuckles and knocked on my head.

"I told you I'm being serious, Abby."

"Well then, Timminy, it's my turn to be serious. I don't care if you're the tallest or the shortest or fattest or skinniest kid in school. I can't *see* you, remember? And it may not have crossed your mind since you're making this all about you, but I happen to be the blindest kid at school, oh yeah, and the blackest kid too, so they tell me. So try to get over yourself, Minny, Timminy, or whatever you want to be called. I don't want to see or hear from you until you do!"

SECRET #16
If you're not careful, you can lose a friend even faster than you made one.

79

CHAPTER 17

WOULD ABBY EVEN talk to me at school? I could hope, couldn't I?

On Tuesday, I didn't see her in the cafeteria when I went to sit at the table with the reading nerds.

I had forgotten to bring anything fun to read so it was me and my math book again (I'd have to scour my shelves to find something, anything, better than a math book). The reading nerds must have towering shelves full of books—they were both reading something new today and had a few spares, just in case. The redhead had all mysteries in his stack, and the other nerd was devouring the Percy Jackson series—reading Book 1 on Friday and, oh man, he was on Book 4 already today.

Finally! I spotted Abby—at the corner table near the door.

Laughing.

Chitchatting.

Popular!

My stomach went all topsy-turvy.

Should I go over to her or not? What if she ignored me? Wait a minute! I knew someone she couldn't ignore . . . Maxi!

Abby really liked Maxi—even if she got angry with *me*. I just needed to find the right Maxi story to tell her. I'd already told her the Maxi-stinks-big-time story. So maybe the Maxi's-vet-appointment-when-we-found-out-she-was-deaf story or the Maxi-chased-the-squirrel-in-circles-and-Roary-roared-by story. Sympathy or drama? Hmm . . .

I finally worked up my courage to go tell Abby the sympathy story. I practiced what I'd say in my head as I inched my way to her corner table. But as I was about to call Abby's name, the kids at her table burst out laughing . . .

"Not again!"

"What a riot!"

"Sounds like back in kindergarten when we . . ."

I turned away as fast as I could. I didn't want to hear about their kindergarten adventures. When you're new to a school, you don't share a kindergarten history with anyone.

I raced back toward the reading nerd table, and— BUMP!

I ran into someone, a *big* someone.

"Watch where you're going, pipsqueak."

"Looking for the squirt table, squirt?"

"We can escort you."

One of the boys I'd dodged in the hall my first day started to pick me up like a baby in his arms. It took all my strength to squirm away from him and race back to the readers' table. Phew! A teacher on duty stood nearby so those big oafs didn't follow me.

The reading nerds didn't even look up as I sat back down. I was as invisible as a ghost sitting there.

I couldn't bear to read any more math so instead I read the ingredients on my apple juice bottle . . . water, apple juice concentrate, ascorbic acid. I kept my head down and pretended to keep reading. What I really wanted was to squeeze myself small enough to fit into that bottle so no one could see me, and then be thrown out with rest of the lunch trash.

SECRET #17

Sometimes you have to throw yourself a pity party.

CHAPTER 18

TWO DAYS LATER, it was Maxi who needed the pity party.

I'd taken her out at dusk to run around a bit before bedtime. She did her business, and then kept walking back and forth on the lawn next to the woods. I figured she was protecting us from wolves, but it wasn't wolves I should have been worried about.

I went to get the shovel from the garage to scoop up her poop, and when I returned, I squinted to see Maxi. It was getting dark, but since she's a big white blob, I was able to spot her on the far side of the lawn.

I hollered, "Maxi, come, girl!"

When would I stop talking to my deaf dog? She may be the deaf one, but *I* was the dumb one. I laughed at myself and walked to fetch her and bring her inside for the night.

But she had started to bark and run after something moving by the edge of the woods.

"No, girl, no! Come back!" I ran too. What was that small, dark blob? I didn't see any white on it, so—*phew*—not a skunk, I hoped.

Maxi was closing in. The small blackish ball was waddling so, so slowly, and something was sticking up. My brain put it all together . . .

A PORCUPINE!

I ran faster and yelled, "STOP, MAXI, STOP!" Then I stopped. She couldn't hear me.

So instead, I shouted, "GO, PORCUPINE, GO!" Figured that made as much sense. Maybe the porcupine was deaf too 'cause he, she, it didn't hear me either. In fact, it *stopped* moving and simply did what porcupines do.

Bristled its back and . . .

HOWL! Poor Maxi had been quilled!

"Maxi, oh, Maxi!" The porcupine moseyed off while Maxi howled and shoved her face into the ground trying to get the quills out. When that didn't work, she tried to dig them off her snout with her paws.

"DAD! MOM! IT'S MAXI!" I don't know what was louder: Maxi's howling or my screaming. We were both so loud I didn't hear the racket in the woods until—

CRASH!

Something burst out of the woods! I screamed louder—

maybe it was a giant mama porcupine coming to quill both of us!

Then I heard, "Oh, you poor puppy." It was Rory! He reached down and scooped up Maxi, who was still clawing at her face.

"Minny, run and have your dad get the car ready. I'll carry your Little Beast out to him."

"Put Maxi down!" I yelled. "We gotta get those quills out of her." I reached up to try to yank out the quills. But when I did, Rory blocked me with his arm.

"Stop it, you Jerk!" I told him. "She's my dog. Let me help her." I reached up again to pluck a quill.

This time Rory didn't block me. Instead he picked me up around the waist and carried me on one hip and Maxi on the other.

"Put me down, Jerk, put me down!" I screamed and tried to hit Rory without hitting Maxi. But he kept carrying both of us. We turned the corner at the front of the garage, and there were my parents all in a panic.

"What's wrong?"

"Why were you screaming?"

"Are you hurt, Timminy?"

"Is Maxi hurt?"

"What did you do, Rory?"

"Pipe down, everyone!" Rory yelled. "Sorry, Mr. AP, but you gotta listen and so does your shrimpy kid."

"Put him down," Dad said.

"Yeah, put me down." It was nice to have Dad sticking up for *me* this time.

"I'll put him down if he stops grabbing at your dog."

"Timminy!" Dad gave me one of those looks. So much for that one second when Dad seemed to be on *my* side. The Jerk put me down and then cradled Maxi in both his arms even as she wriggled to get rid of the quills.

Dad looked Rory right in the eye and said, "You have one minute. Go."

"Your puppy lost a battle with a porcupine. She's hurting, but you can't pull quills out like Minny here keeps trying to do. They're barbed, they'll break off, leave pieces inside her, get infected."

"So what do you suggest?" Dad asked.

"Take her to the emergency clinic in Bangor. They'll pull 'em out the right way."

"But Maxi has a vet right here in town," said Mom.

"Closed at night. If you call their number, they'll have a message referring you to the Bangor place," said Rory.

"Got it. Thanks, Rory. Lynda, you drive. I'll hold Maxi in the backseat. Timminy, look up the clinic's number and tell them we're on our way. Then send us the clinic's address. After that, call Abby's parents. Their number is on the fridge. Just so they know you're here alone if you need them."

"Dad, no! I'm going. Maxi is *my* dog."

"Not this time, Timminy. You have a job—those calls. They're important too. Plus there's school tomorrow. We don't know how late we'll be."

Ew! I wished I were as little as everyone thought I was so I could throw a toddler temper tantrum. But I'd failed Maxi already that night. I couldn't get in the way of her getting help. So I simply said, "Yes, sir."

"Good boy," Dad said to me.

And then "Good girl," as he reached to take Maxi from Rory.

But Rory held on to her and said, "Get in the back, Mr. AP, buckle up, and I'll pass her to you."

Dad got in and as Rory passed Maxi to him, Dad said, "Thanks for your help. Stop in my office in the morning and I'll let you know how she's doing."

"I will and no problem, Mr. AP."

Dad nodded as Mom drove off.

"You okay, kid?" asked Rory.

"Yeah."

"Want me to stay?"

"No! You're *not* staying."

"Okay then, I'd better head back." He started down the driveway.

"But you came out of the woods," I said.

"Yeah, out for a walk, but it's kinda dark to go back

that way. Don't want to run into that porcupine and need you to come rescue me. You might have a hard time carrying me to the clinic." He snorted at his joke.

I was too tired to put up with Rory so I turned to go inside.

But the Jerk wasn't finished. "Did I hear your puppy's name right? Maxi?"

I nodded.

"Aww! Minny and Maxi, how cute."

I went inside and slammed the door before my parents would have to come visit me in jail for assault and battery—below the knees!

SECRET #18
Trouble is easier to get *into* than out of.

CHAPTER 19

NOW I KNEW what a worried parent felt like. I couldn't stop pacing and checking the clock.

Mr. Winslow asked if I wanted him to come over and keep me company, but I said "no thanks." I was a big kid, a fifth grader. I'd stayed home alone before. Why did everyone think I was such a wimpy little kid?

But if Abby had offered to come over, I'd have said yes in a second. Abby cared about Maxi, even though she'd only just met her. She would understand why I was so worried. But she also had common *sense* that I didn't have, so she could talk me out of my worst fears . . .

Maxi would die.

Maxi's snout would get infected and have to be amputated. Then she couldn't hear or *smell*.

Maxi would be in the pet hospital for a week, a month, a *year*!

Maxi would be too scared to go outside the rest of her

life, and she'd have to use one of those embarrassing kitty litter boxes. And I'd have to *clean* it!

But mostly, Maxi would die . . .

My parents got home shortly after midnight. Maxi was still groggy from the anesthesia they'd put her under to remove the quills. Dad carried her into the living room and put her on her bed. For the first time, she wasn't going to be the watchdog in the hallway outside our bedrooms. Which was okay by me. It was my turn to guard her. After my parents went to bed, I snuck downstairs and lay next to Maxi. I rested my hand on her side as I repeated my mind words.

It's okay, girl. Okay. Okay.

I'm sorry. Sorry. Sorry.

I'll never let anything bad happen to you again. Never. Never.

Her breathing was so even, so peaceful—she didn't even whimper with her usual puppy dreams. I tried to stay awake to comfort her all night long, but instead, touching her, feeling the rhythm of her breaths put *me* to sleep.

When Dad gently squeezed my shoulder to wake me in the morning, he didn't crab at me for sleeping downstairs. He said, "Looks like you both had a good night's sleep." I looked at Maxi and smiled. We each had left matching drool spots on her dog bed.

Maxi was still sleeping when I left with Dad for school. Mom was going to juggle her schedule so she could stay home with Maxi, who needed to take antibiotic pills for a few days to stop any infection. Lucky puppy—her pills were going to be hidden in chunks of cheese.

When I got to school, I couldn't focus. I just wanted to get back home to Maxi and make sure she was okay.

I peeked into Dad's office before lunch. I knew he would have checked in with Mom. He was busy talking to a teacher, but I caught his eye and mouthed, *Maxi*. He kept talking while giving me a thumbs-up. I smiled and nodded.

In the lunchroom, I got hot lunch for the first time, since I'd woken up too late to pack a lunch. As I walked with my tray past Abby's table, she was busy chatting with her friends and ed tech. She acted like nothing was wrong. Maybe her dad hadn't told her about my call last night. Should I tell her Maxi got quilled? She didn't care about *me*, but I knew she cared about Maxi. But everyone else was there, and I didn't want to step in the middle of their conversation.

So I sat at my usual table and kept staring at Abby as I pushed the food around on my tray.

She'd want to know.

She wouldn't.

She'd want to know.

She wouldn't.

I needed a scientific way to figure this out . . .

So I spun my fork on the table. If the tines pointed toward Abby, she'd want to know. If they pointed away from Abby, she wouldn't want to know.

On the first spin the tines pointed away from Abby so . . .

I did two out of three.

The second spin pointed toward Abby.

And the third pointed . . .

Toward Abby.

I had my scientific answer—Abby *definitely* wanted to know about Maxi and the porcupine.

But how to tell her?

I didn't want everyone at her table to know. Just her.

If I stopped to talk, her friends might ask, "Who's the midget, Abby?" I could write her a note, but I didn't know how to write in braille.

Hmm.

Lightbulb moment!

Abby had a helper at school for a reason—to help her! I'd write a note and give it to Abby's ed tech to read to her. Then Abby would call me the second school finished to hear all about Maxi's quilling.

I found a pen, but I didn't have any paper unless I ripped pages out of the nerds' books. I didn't want them kicking me off their table so my napkin would have to do. On one side I wrote . . .

Abby's Ed Tech,

 Please read the note on the other side just to
Abby. Thank you!

Then on the other side, I wrote . . .

Abby,

 Maxi got quilled by a porcupine last night. She
wanted you to know, but her penmanship is
<u>PAWful</u> ☺! She's going to be okay . . . PROBABLY.

Your neighbor,
Timminy

I reread it twice, then a third time. It was short, simple, to the point, and a *little* funny—I hoped—to make
Abby laugh.

 I stood up and took such a deep breath I hiccupped. I
kept hiccupping as I carried my lunch tray and the note.
I walked toward the return-tray drop-off, eyeing Abby
the whole way, then stopped behind her ed tech, and
whispered, "Excuse me—here." I dropped the napkin
note in front of the ed tech and hiccupped my loudest
hiccup yet.

 The ed tech jumped, which made me jump, which
made my tray jump out of my hands and land . . . upside
down . . .

On top of her head!

A mac-and-cheese-peas-applesauce shampoo!

"Ew!" The ed tech squealed, grabbing my napkin note to wipe food out of her hair.

"OH NO!" *HICCUP!*

"Ew!" the ed tech kept squealing. "Ew!"

"STOP!" I screamed.

I grabbed the slimy napkin from the ed tech and said, "Don't wipe with this—*hiccup*—it's a note for Abby!" *Hiccup!*

"Timminy? Is that you?" asked Abby.

"It's some peewee kid," said a boy.

"That's Timminy." Abby nodded.

Other kids at the table jumped into the conversation.

"A note for Abby?"

"She can't read it."

"She's blind!"

But before I could explain, the ed tech squealed, "Ew! My hair! Aaargh! I just had it done!"

I wished some of that food had gotten into the ed tech's mouth to plug it. She groaned again.

"Oh, shut up already! I'm sorry."

"Timminy!" Abby gasped.

I opened my mouth to explain to her, to her friends, to her ed tech that this was all just one big mix-up.

HICCUP!

"OH, FORGET IT!" I yelled and stomped out of the cafeteria.

SECRET #19
A good idea can turn bad faster than the time it takes you to hiccup.

CHAPTER 20

I WANTED OUT of this school. *Now!*

But how?

I ducked into the bathroom.

I knew I couldn't stall in a stall all day.

I'd probably fit through that tiny frosted bathroom window, but it was too high, near the ceiling. I couldn't reach it, and I wasn't about to holler for the Jerk to come and give me a boost.

I could only think of one thing that *might* work. I ran the hot water in the faucet and rubbed it on my face and neck. Then I half walked, half ran down the hall to the office. I muttered to the secretary, "I'm sick. Need to see my dad, er . . . Mr. Harris."

"Why don't you go see the school nurse, Timminy?"

"She can't fix what's wrong with me."

Then that softie secretary said, "Have a seat. I'll see if he's available."

Dad stepped out of his office and waved me in. "What's wrong? Are you okay?"

"No, I'm sick. I need to go home."

He felt my forehead. "I don't think you have a temp, but you do feel kind of clammy. Any other symptoms?"

"I think I could puke." Which wasn't a lie.

Dad continued, "Why don't you lie down in the nurse's office or sit in here for a while to see if you'll feel better? Maybe it's something you ate at lunch."

It was lunch all right, but *not* anything I ate.

"Dad, I need to go home. *Please!*"

"Okay, I'll see if Mom can come pick you up."

"But should she leave Maxi alone? So soon?"

"I'll call her."

I could only hear Dad's side of the conversation, but I could fill in the rest. They both thought I was "worried sick" about Maxi, which was fine with me if it got me out of school.

Mom did come pick me up and—surprise!—Maxi was in the backseat. "Oh, you're doing better, girl." She cuddled up on the ride home, practically climbing into my lap.

I buried my face in Maxi's fur and whispered, "I feel better already."

SECRET #20
Sometimes the best medicine isn't medicine at all.

CHAPTER 21

"I'M HOME TO take care of you now, girl."

I was relieved Maxi didn't seem to have any leftover problems from the run-in with the porcupine, and that she didn't even hold a grudge against me. I rubbed her belly and snuck her some cheese *without* pills. Then we both had another drool nap.

When I woke up, there was . . .

ABBY!

I jumped up, wiped the drool off my face, and said, "Who let you in?"

"Your mom. Nice to see you too, Timminy."

"It's just I'm sick, Abby. You don't want to catch my germs."

"You're not sick. You're embarrassed about what happened at lunch. It can feel like it, but you won't actually die from embarrassment."

"Are you sure?"

"Ninety-nine percent sure. Of course, there's always the chance you're special and belong to the one percent who will die."

She was right . . . if I was part of the 0.001 percentile for height, then I probably was part of the one percent who'd die of embarrassment. But I wasn't going to tell Abby that—she'd think I was making it all about *me* again.

When I didn't answer, Abby said, "Maybe you are sick. Your funny bone seems to be broken."

Then she slid her cane along the floor until it bumped Maxi. Maxi woke up, saw Abby, wagged her tail ninety miles an hour, then jumped up and smothered her with slobbery kisses.

"Well, at least someone's glad to see me. And I'm glad to see you too, girl. Are you okay?" Maxi kept up the kisses. "I'll take that as a yes. Is she really okay, Timminy?"

"Yeah."

"When I got home from school today, my dad told me about your call last night and what happened to Maxi. I told him he was a day too late filling me in. Parents!" Abby sighed. "He should have known I'd want him to bring me over last night to be sure Maxi was all right."

This time I smiled. Forks don't lie. I *knew* Abby would want to know.

Maxi kept kissing Abby, but she paused at her eyes, gently sniffed, and gave them "love licks" (or, at least, that's what it looked like to me).

I smiled. "She knows something's wrong with your eyes."

"Yeah," said Abby, "she gives them the softest kisses, like she wants to heal them or something."

"Why aren't you wearing your dark glasses?" I realized something was missing.

Abby coughed. "I thought if you saw my eyes, maybe you'd remember I'm blind and can't read notes."

"Not funny, Abby. I *know* you're blind. The note wasn't for you to read—it was for your ed tech to read to you, to let you know about Maxi's run-in with the porcupine."

Abby burst out laughing. "I would have given anything to have seen the food shower you gave Mrs. Russell."

"I didn't mean to."

"I know, but still, I wish I could have seen it." Abby laughed again.

The echo of everyone laughing at me during the lunch fiasco filled my brain. It made me embarrassed all over again.

"If all you want to do is laugh at me," I said, "you can leave."

"Actually, I can't go until I call my dad to come get me. He dropped me off, and I refuse to play dodge car because you're feeling sorry for yourself again."

"I'm not feeling sorry! Jeez! You make me *so angry*!"

"Good! I'm glad. Anger is better than self-pity."

"Actually, I wish *I* were the one who was blind so you'd just disappear!"

Abby jumped in, "Well, I wish I were deaf like Maxi so I couldn't hear all your whining!"

WOOF! WOOF! WOOF!

Maxi started barking like crazy.

First at me.

Then at Abby.

Me.

Abby.

Back and forth.

As if she were scolding us. It worked—we shut up.

"Sorry, girl," we said.

WOOF! WOOF! WOOF!

Maxi wouldn't let it go.

WOOF! WOOF! WOOF!

Mom opened the den door. "What's wrong with Maxi? I'm trying to get some work done and it's hard with this noise. Does she need to go outside?"

"Sorry, Mom. I'll take her out."

"Keep her out of trouble this time and don't let her off her leash. Understand?"

"Yeah, Mom. No more porcupine adventures."

"Good," said Mom, heading back into the den.

I grabbed Maxi's leash and asked Abby, "Wanna come?"

"To finish our argument? Sure." But as she stood and

followed, sliding her cane side to side, she hit one of Maxi's toys and it bounced in front of her foot.

"Watch . . ." But before I got "out" *out* of my mouth, Abby tripped, lost her balance, and fell.

"Are you hurt?" I asked.

"Just my pride." Abby grinned.

"I would say I know how that feels, but I won't before you whack me with your cane and accuse me of whining again."

I reached out. "My hand is in front of your left hand. Hang on and I'll help you up." But before I could, Maxi decided it was time for a pig pile. She jumped on Abby and started wrestling with her.

"Maxi, NO!" I said.

"It's okay," said Abby as she play-wrestled with Maxi. I got down on the floor and joined the fun. I was starting to realize Abby Winslow wasn't exactly breakable.

WOOF! WOOF! WOOF! Maxi was getting rowdy.

Mom opened the door again. "Out! All of you!" She pointed toward the sliding doors.

"Sorry," I said.

"Me too," Abby said.

WOOF! WOOF! WOOF! Maxi said, not sounding the least bit sorry.

SECRET #21
Some things aren't as fragile as they seem.

102

CHAPTER 22

"HANG ON TO my arm," I said to Abby as she, Maxi, and I all made our way outside. "Three steps down," I continued. "There's a railing on your left or you can hold on to my arm."

Abby hung on to me until we were standing on the lawn.

"Phew! We made it!" she said. "The short one led the deaf and blind ones. I'm impressed."

"Yeah, right," I said.

"No, really. Most people won't jump in and start leading me without being asked. Plus you were dealing with Maxi too. That's a lot to juggle."

I looked closer at Abby's facial expression to see if she was teasing me. It's trickier reading a face without eye clues—I'd never realized how much eyes show our feelings. Abby wasn't smirking, and her nose wasn't scrunched, so I didn't think she was teasing me. I took a chance and said, "So, I really did okay?"

"Really good for the first time—you gave clear directions, were sure of yourself, but . . ."

"I *knew* there was going to be a *but*. What'd I do wrong?"

"Nothing wrong," said Abby. "Just some things you could do to be more helpful. I'll show you."

"Wait a minute. Let me walk Maxi around to do her business first."

"Then you can help me with my *blind business*." Abby smiled and sat on the bottom step to wait.

It didn't take Maxi long to sniff out a perfect spot for *her* business.

"Let me scoop this poop before you teach me how to be a better guide dog."

Abby stood up. "No, wait. Leave it there. It'll be a real obstacle you can guide me around. No doggie doo-doo on the shoes, please!" Abby laughed.

I hooked Maxi's leash to the rail, and she was happy to lie on the cool grass while Abby stood up and reached for my arm.

"Don't you want your cane too?" I asked, seeing she'd left it on the steps.

"No, either someone leads me or I use my cane. It would be too confusing to process information from your movements plus my cane. Walk beside me, but a half step ahead too, so I can follow your lead." Abby held on to my elbow and said, "Get moving."

"Aye-aye." I laughed, but then shut up and concentrated. I didn't want to mess up. I'd already messed up too many things with Abby.

I walked slowly, around obstacles—trees, bushes, Maxi's outside toys—does every puppy have that many toys?—and her poop pile.

"How am I doing?" I asked.

"Not bad. I haven't stepped in anything gross yet. But you can go faster—we're not slugs."

I picked up my pace and confidence. "Better?"

"Yeah, now let's try some ninety-degree turns. Before turning, stop moving, and say 'right' or 'left,' then turn and I'll follow. Try to lead me through some trickier places too—where I have to duck my head or follow directly behind you."

I laughed. "You're one brave girl, Abby Winslow. You realize I've never had to duck my head, not once in my whole life."

"You'd better tell *me* to duck or tree branches will poke my eyes out."

"Ewww! That's gross."

"I know," said Abby, smiling proudly.

I shook my head and said, "Okay. Hang on for your life." And she did.

I guided Abby through ninety-degree turns and then

into the woods, under branches—"Duck, Abby, duck!" Between close-together trees, moving my guiding arm behind my back, as Abby directed me, so she'd know it was narrow and would have to walk behind me instead of beside me. Things were fine until she stumbled on a tree root and scraped her arm on another tree. "I'm bleeding," she said, then giggled.

"That makes you happy because?"

"Because I love being out in these woods. It makes me feel alive. And losing a little blood is no big deal."

"If you say so."

"Timminy, get my cane."

"Why?"

"Because now I want to make my way out of the woods without your help—only using my cane."

"You're talking crazy again."

"Just get it—please."

"I don't feel good about this," I told Abby. "I couldn't protect my deaf dog from a porcupine last night. I don't want to be responsible for a skunk spraying or a moose charging my blind friend."

Abby smiled. "Glad you realize we're friends. And, um, friends do friends favors, like bringing your poor helpless blind friend her cane."

"Oh, Abby, you may not see with your eyes, but, boy oh boy, you clearly *see* how to get what you want. Stay put until I get back."

When I gave her cane to her, she said, "Thanks. You can leave now."

I sighed and said, "Bye." I made a big show of stomping away, and then ducked behind a tree to be nearby in case Abby needed me.

Abby still didn't move. "I'm not taking a single step until you get out of here and back on the steps with Maxi."

"Abby, I can't get away with anything when you're around."

"Right! And don't forget that. Now go!"

I came out of the woods and sat on the bottom step, hugging Maxi as I listened for Abby. I could hear her cane stirring up dried leaves on the ground, and it sounded like she stumbled once. But as I listened carefully and waited to hear her fall (then I'd *have* to go help her no matter what she'd said), there was no crashing sound. Wait! What if I couldn't hear her because she was walking the wrong way, away from our yard, deeper into the woods?

Just as I'd convinced myself I needed to go rescue Abby, she came walking out of the woods with the biggest smile on her face.

She made it back to the steps, leaned down to pat Maxi, got some puppy kisses, and said, "I've lived here since I was a baby, and this is the first time I've ever walked in these woods alone. I did it!"

"You did."

"Now you do it!" Abby said.

"What do you mean?"

Abby bit her bottom lip and her voice grew quieter. "Walk with my cane and close your eyes."

"I'm not sure . . ."

"Oh, never mind," Abby said.

I grabbed the cane from her and said, "Why not? The worst that can happen is I'll get myself into a messy situation. It won't be the first time."

Abby laughed.

I closed my eyes and started walking away. It didn't take long to figure out I had to hold the cane below the top grip since I was shorter than Abby.

Slowly, so, so slowly, I moved the cane from side to side, shoulder distance width, with a sweeping motion, as Abby had done. When I felt something with the cane, I paused, trying to conjure up a mind map of my backyard, then steered my steps away from whatever I'd touched. I listened for Maxi's panting, Abby's breathing, as anchors to know where *safe* was. I was much slower than Abby. When I lost my balance, my eyes popped opened. I felt like a cheater as I shut them again (Abby didn't have that option!).

When I finally felt Maxi with the cane, I leaned down for some puppy kisses. It was like she was congratulating me—"You did it, my boy."

"Not bad," said Abby. "At least it sounded like you did all right."

"It took lots of concentration, and I felt nervous the whole time."

Suddenly, Maxi whined.

"It's okay, girl. We're done with our adventures. Time to give you some attention."

But as I went to get one of Maxi's toys, Abby said, "She's whining because she wants a turn."

"Maxi is *not* walking with your cane."

"That's not what I meant, Timminy. Let me hold her leash and have her be my guide dog for a few minutes."

"You're talking a little crazy again. You want the deaf one to lead the blind one?"

"Better than the blind one leading the deaf one." Abby laughed. "Between the two of us, we'll have all five senses covered, won't we, girl?" She leaned down to Maxi and got a couple of enthusiastic slurps.

"But she's not trained as a guide dog, Abby. Obedience is *not* her strength, and I don't think it's only because she's deaf. It's a Great Pyrenees trait."

"Don't worry—you'll be right here watching us. I won't let go of her leash—no matter what. And we'll stay on the lawn. No woods."

"You really love pushing the limits, don't you?"

"When your world's small, you've gotta push or it'll keep getting smaller and smaller."

I didn't have an answer to that, so I led Maxi by her leash with one hand and Abby by my other hand to the middle of the lawn. I put the leash in Abby's hand, lifted Maxi's snout to look her in the eyes, and pointed forward. "Go, girl. Be easy. It's Abby."

Maxi took three steps forward. Abby followed. Maxi looked back at me, then Abby, for permission to continue. I hesitated, but Abby shook the leash as if it were a rein for a horse and said, "Go, girl."

Maxi did. She led Abby slowly, step by step, across the lawn. But when she approached the edge of the woods and the spot where the porcupine had quilled her, she whined and walked in a circle, around and around Abby, winding her up with the leash.

"Aaaaah!" screamed Abby. "She tied me up. It was working. What happened?"

I couldn't stop laughing.

"Timminy, what's going on?"

"She's . . . trying to keep you from going into the woods and getting quilled. It's her Great Pyrenees's instincts. She circles us whenever she's trying to keep us safe."

I was still laughing as I unwound Maxi and her leash from Abby. Then I turned Maxi away from the woods and pointed her toward the house.

I told Abby I'd see her back at the steps and ran off. Usually whenever I'd run, Maxi would sprint after me—a game of chase. But this time, she didn't run; instead she guided Abby ever so slowly back to the steps, back to me.

I didn't think it was possible, but Abby's big smile, which I had seen when she walked out of the woods alone, grew even bigger.

"You did it," I said.

I swear Abby's eyes were smiling, too, as she nodded and said, "We did it."

SECRET #22
It's better to focus on what you *can* do instead of what you *can't* do.

CHAPTER 23

BEFORE ABBY LEFT, she made me promise to sit with her at lunch on Monday.

"But I didn't think you wanted me around."

"I don't if you're going to act like a whining toddler."

"And if I do?"

"Then you're going to sit in time-out." Abby smirked.

"But won't your friends tease me about the note? And won't your ed tech start screaming again when she sees me?"

"I'll explain everything to them and warn Mrs. Russell to wear a poncho for protection when you're around."

"Abby!"

"Kidding—sort of. So my friends will tease you—that's what friends do, just like I teased you now."

"I'll think about it."

Abby ignored me and talked to Maxi. "Bark some sense into that boy of yours."

On cue, Maxi barked.

I wanted to whine, "Two against one is not fair."

Saturday was a big day for Maxi, because Mom was taking her to her first obedience class. I begged to go, but Mom said the instructor wanted only one person in charge of each puppy. At our house we all knew Mom was the Boss. She promised to teach Dad and me everything she learned in class. She also cautioned us: "Remember, it's not an obedience class for deaf dogs—they don't have one around here, not any in the state of Maine, I don't think. It's just for regular puppies—so don't expect miracles. But I'll combine what I learn there with some sign language I know." We all agreed we had to try something, anything to get Maxi to understand us and follow our directions so she'd be safer. The porcupine run-in had scared us.

While Mom was gone, I looked for my own way to help Maxi. I shut myself in my room and searched the internet . . .

deaf dog obedience
deaf dog training
deaf dog safety

There were all kinds of ways to keep a deaf dog safe. Maybe a fence, like Abby's, that could protect Maxi and stop prickly porcupines from wandering into our yard (and Big Jerks too). There were invisible electric fences that keep dogs within certain boundaries. Best of all, I learned about pager collars, which vibrate and send a signal to get your dog's attention. This was exciting—the pager collars looked like they might be the answer to Maxi being a free puppy.

My stomach flip-flopped when I found a bunch of videos of deaf dogs. It helped seeing that Maxi wasn't the only deaf dog in the world (maybe next I'd search *short boy video*—no one wants to be the only one).

I also checked out videos of blind people walking with canes and with guide dogs, which led me to the MIRA Foundation. Oh man, MIRA could be Abby's MIRAcle answer—they let kids Abby's age get guide dogs. I needed to research it more before telling Abby. Didn't want to get her hopes up for nothing. But if it worked out, and she got a guide dog *sooner*, I'd be her best friend for life!

I bookmarked the pages about the collars and MIRA to read later, since I really should have been doing my homework.

Why was reading about dogs on the internet so much more interesting than reading about acids and bases and writing a report on Harry "Handcuff" Houdini?

I'd much rather learn about the stuff I could really use in my life.

"We're back!" Mom yelled.

I hurried downstairs to see how Maxi made out with her first class. Hopefully she didn't get kicked out of school already.

I sat on the floor, rubbing Maxi's belly, as Mom filled Dad and me in. Mom was excited. Maxi just burped.

"What's that smell?" I asked.

"Horseradish cheese. They used what motivated each dog. For Maxi it's food."

Dad and I looked at each other. "Duh!"

Then Dad asked, "So we've gotta buy stock in a horseradish cheese factory?"

Mom rolled her eyes. "No, Kenneth. And we're not using horseradish cheese when we train her at home. If we use cheese all the time, Maxi will gain too much weight. They have bite-size training treats that come in different flavors. We can pick some up at the pet shop."

It sounded like Mom had things figured out. Way to take charge!

Dad and I listened and Maxi burped a few more stinky burps as Mom told us they'd first had the puppies socialize with each other. Sounded like a puppy playdate to me.

Then they encouraged puppies to watch their humans as they focused on two commands: "sit" and "stay." There was a hand signal for each command. Mom showed us. For sit, we had to move our open palm down by our leg and then raise it up to our shoulders. For stay, it was common sense—an open hand in front of her snout like a traffic cop would do (the same as the FedEx driver had done with Maxi).

Mom said, "The key is consistency." She made us practice each gesture a couple of times and then we all agreed to focus on those two commands with Maxi until she learned something new at next week's class.

"You're going to be a star student, girl. I know it." I kissed Maxi's snout as she belched another horseradish cheese burp right in my face.

SECRET #23
Learning is a lot more fun when it's stuff you care about.

CHAPTER 24

FIRST THING MONDAY morning, Ms. Sanborn said, "Sorry, Timminy, but I've decided I'm kicking you out to wait with the other students until the homeroom bell rings."

"Why? What'd I do wrong?"

She smiled. "Nothing. And I've enjoyed getting to know you these past two weeks, but I realized I haven't been doing you any favors letting you hang out in homeroom for such a long time every morning."

"That's not true, Ms. Sanborn. I'm glad you've let me stay in here. I know it's been a few years since you went to middle school, but it's a scary world out there."

"My point exactly, Timminy. When I was a kid growing up, my dad was career army. I changed schools more often than some people change the oil in their cars. It was easier to hang out with teachers than to always be the new kid and face the other students. I turned out mostly normal, but I still have a fear of new situations. I don't want to be responsible for any of your future phobias."

"What about my present phobias?" I asked.

"Very funny, Timminy. Now out with you. I'll see you again when the homeroom bell rings and we can say good morning all over again."

Why did everyone think I was joking when I wasn't?

As soon as I stepped outside, it started.

The buzz, the whispers, the stares.

And it wasn't just the usual *short* digs. I kept overhearing conversations about lunch on Friday . . .

"Dumped the whole tray."

"Passed a note . . ."

"How could he not know . . ."

". . . dumb, dumber, *dumbest*!"

I felt like I was inside a pinball machine as I ricocheted away from conversation after conversation, but there was no place to escape.

I put my head down and hurried to the cafeteria to wait for the homeroom bell. But as I stepped through the door, I heard a sudden burst of laughter. Not a good idea to return to the scene of the crime. I did a U-turn and slipped into the bathroom, locked myself in a stall, and stood on the toilet seat so my feet wouldn't show below if anyone looked—and fortunately, in my case, I was so short my head wouldn't show above the stall. The only thing I had to worry about was keeping my balance and not falling into the toilet.

I finally heard the homeroom bell and listened to make certain there was no one else still in the bathroom. I didn't want to be so late I'd have to get a pass from the office to get back into homeroom, so I quickly stopped at my locker to grab a couple of books. I'd almost made it, when . . .

BAM!

Shoved inside!

SLAM!

Everything dark!

I listened. Heard big feet running away, and then nothing—no voices, no footsteps, no other lockers slamming.

Everyone was in homeroom, except *me*.

Now what?

I had no clue how to open a locker from the inside. (Heck, I'd had a hard enough time opening my locker from the outside.)

I'd wanted to hide and now I got my wish. Maybe I should stay put and they'd find me in a week or two after my body started to smell. Oh man, I sounded grosser than Abby and her poking-her-eyeballs-out talk.

Abby! If I didn't make it out of this locker, I'd miss

lunch with her and her friends. I wasn't sure how many more mess-ups I'd get before she ditched me as a friend, put me in a box, and mailed me back to Portland.

How could I get out? Maybe I should have worked harder on my Harry Houdini report and learned some of his escape tricks. I shook the back side of the lock to see if it'd give. No luck. I used the zipper on my jacket to try to pick the lock. Still no luck. When all else fails . . .

SCREAM!

Maybe Kassy would be on her way back from a student council meeting. Or magic-touch boy would appear instead of disappear. Or Ms. Sanborn would miss me in homeroom and come looking for me and apologize for sending me out into this dangerous world.

I paused. Didn't hear anything so I screamed again.

The door started shaking and opened. *Phew!*

"Thanks."

But I looked up and changed it to "no thanks."

It was the Beast Roary.

"Want me to shut you back inside?" he asked.

"Like you did before?"

"Wasn't me."

"Yeah, right," I said.

"I heard you scream when I walked by. But I can jam you back inside if that's what you want, Minny."

He started to shove me.

"Stop!" I wanted to say more, but didn't. I wasn't ready to move back into my locker tomb.

I slammed my locker, started down the hall, then spun around, and yelled to Rory. "Wait! How'd you know my locker combination?"

He turned back and laughed. "I don't. I can jimmy open any locker. Learned it back when I was a fifth-grade pipsqueak like you."

I walked up to him and looked up, way up. "You were never a pipsqueak. More like the Beast of the East."

"You're right. Not a pipsqueak like you, Minny. You win the pipsqueak prize." He snorted and added, "Hey! What'd you call me?"

Uh-oh, why had I pushed my luck? I mumbled, "Beast of the East."

Rory snorted a bigger snort. I dodged sideways in case any flying debris came out of his nose.

"I like that," he said. "Maine's east. I'm a beast. Think that's what I'm gonna start calling myself."

"Go for it," I said, forcing a laugh. Who calls *themselves* a nickname? Weird. But since he liked it, I said, "See you around, Beast of the East."

Rory slapped me on the back—almost knocked the wind out of me—and said, "Thanks. I owe you. For the name. I'll show you how to jimmy open a locker tomorrow before school, in case anyone shoves you inside again. Meet me at your locker when the buses get here."

Brrrrrrng!

The bell. Homeroom period was already over, and I never even made it to homeroom.

"Ugh," I said. "Now I've gotta go get a pass from the office to get into my first-period class."

"Me too—and I just came from your dad's office. Why does everyone always blame us big guys for trouble on the bus?"

"Yeah, you're the innocent Beast of the East." I smirked.

"That's right! Come on, let's go."

Just the way to make my dad's day. Rory and I skipping into his office together for class passes.

SECRET #24

Just when you think you've got people figured out, they surprise you and you have to go back to the drawing, er . . . "figuring out" board.

CHAPTER 25

I ARRIVED IN the cafeteria and saw there was an empty spot on either side of Abby. It looked like she was saving me a place.

Should I or shouldn't I?

I'd survived the day so far—sort of. I hadn't died from everyone talking about me before school. I wasn't still a prisoner inside my locker. And Dad had given me a pass to class, simply saying, "We'll talk . . . *later*." I wasn't sure I'd survive later.

Sooooo I took a deep breath and said, "Hi, Abby. Okay if I sit down?"

Abby smiled and nodded, but didn't say anything.

I guessed she wasn't going to make this any easier, so it was up to me.

"Hi, everyone. I'm Timminy, your lunchtime entertainment."

Abby's friends looked at one another and burst out laughing. Abby, loudest of all.

"Hi, I'm Brian. Oh man, Timminy, that was so funny on Friday. Made me bust a gut."

"Did you see Mrs. Russell's face when you dumped the food on her?" one wide-eyed girl asked softly.

"I didn't mean to . . ."

The girl blushed. "My name is Devon. I'm sure you didn't, but—"

Before anyone could say anything else, Mrs. Russell herself sat down on the other side of Abby and stared.

At me.

"I'm Timminy Harris, Abby's new neighbor," I said.

"I know who you are." She turned her attention to Abby. "Let me help you butter your roll, dear."

Abby put her hand over Mrs. Russell's. "I've been buttering my own bread since I was three years old. Might have been a little messy, but—"

"We don't need messy at school." Mrs. Russell snatched Abby's roll and buttered it.

We all looked at one another.

A-W-K-W-A-R-D!

Leave it to Abby to break the silence.

"Hey, did I tell you guys Timminy and I were introduced to each other by his puppy, Maxi—who is the cutest thing evah! Don't take my word for it though— I'm blind."

Everyone laughed, except Mrs. Russell.

I followed her lead. "Yeah, wanna see? She's a Great Pyrenees." Like a proud parent I always carried a photo of Maxi, so I pulled it out and passed it around the table. They all *ooh*-ed and *aww*-ed. Even Mrs. Russell's face thawed a tiny bit.

But when I told them Maxi was deaf, they gasped.

"You're kidding." A girl named Becca shook her head.

"Poor thing." Mrs. Russell clicked her tongue.

"How's she survive?" asked Brian, scratching his head.

Abby cleared her throat. "The same way I survive. We disabled creatures make do somehow."

"True," Becca said softly as she glanced down.

"Yes, somehow we manage." Abby lifted her hand up to her forehead as if she were a damsel in distress. So dramatic. We all cracked up.

I smiled at Maxi's photo before putting it away. *Thanks, girl, for helping me fit in. Maybe you'll get to meet Abby's friends. Sounds like they'd like to meet you.*

"And you, Timminy?"

Ugh. I got caught with my mind wandering and had no idea what Mrs. Russell was talking about. I was surprised she was even talking to me.

Might as well 'fess up. "Sorry, I was still thinking about Maxi."

Mrs. Russell repeated her question. "What do you want to be when you grow up? An assistant principal like your father?"

"Let me think . . ." Why'd she have to bring up my dad? It was hard enough fitting in without having his shadow join us for lunch.

Mrs. Russell said, "Never mind. It is a hard qu—"

"Got it," I interrupted her. "What do I want to be when I grow up?" I paused until everyone was looking at me, plus to drive Mrs. Russell crazy. "Tall. I want to be tall."

Everyone laughed. Devon even shot milk out her nose as she laughed, then hid her face in her hands.

"Gross!"

"Yuck!"

Abby sighed. "What happened? What'd I miss?"

Mrs. Russell said, "Nothing, Abby."

I said, "Mrs. Russell, I know you're new working with Abby, but it's time you learned blind talk. Abby couldn't see what happened that made us laugh, so could you describe it to her? 'Cause it really *was* something."

Mrs. Russell shifted in her seat and began to get up. "Um, er . . ." She'd seen the milk snot—almost got sprayed by it. "I have some paperwork to do before your next class, Abby. I'll be back to get you when the bell rings."

Abby spoke up. "Never mind, Mrs. Russell. Timminy will lead me to class."

"That's not allowed. It's my job," said Mrs. Russell.

"Sure it's allowed," said Abby. "Timminy has guided me before. Are you saying you don't trust the assistant principal's son?"

Mrs. Russell stammered, "It-it's not that. It's j-just . . . oh, never mind." She walked off—couldn't escape fast enough.

When Mrs. Russell was gone, Abby held up her hand and said, "High-five, Timminy."

Then we all jumped into blind talk, trying to describe to Abby the milk-out-the-nose trick she'd missed and trying to one-up one another, except for Devon—she blushed and didn't say a word.

"It was like a glue gun squirting from a face."

"More like a zit being popped without even having to be squeezed."

"A slimy grub—that white wormy thing—being shot like a cannon from your nostril."

"A juicy fart escaping from your nose, instead of your butt."

We laughed like crazy. Good thing the bell rang before the teacher on cafeteria duty had to give us a warning.

I hadn't realized how complicated lunch was at Abby's table. They were already sitting down when I got there, but now that everyone was getting up to leave, I realized this didn't all magically happen.

"You lead Abby to class," Becca said to me. "And I'll bring her lunch tray back."

"And I've got your tray and Devon's," said Brian as he picked one up in each hand while balancing his own tray on top of them.

Then I saw Devon stand awkwardly and grab a couple of short metal crutches for walking. They had parts that hooked to her lower arms. I tried not to stare, but I hadn't even noticed Devon had a problem with her legs. Man, I still had a lot to learn about Abby's friends. But first thing first. I turned toward Abby and offered her my arm. "My elbow is in front of your left hand." I told her.

We set off down the hall. I wasn't sure where Abby's classroom was, so she had to tell me. I'd hoped we could talk on the way, but I found I had to really concentrate on leading her through the hallway, with kids darting and dodging every which way without warning. It was much trickier than leading her in my wide-open backyard.

Mrs. Russell was tapping her foot when we got there. "You made it," she said.

"Of course," said Abby. "Timminy's a good guide." Then she turned to me. "You really are. Thanks for the escort. Talk to you later."

I had so much to talk about with Abby, but I simply said, "Later."

"Yes, later," a deeper voice echoed. "Be ready."

I turned. It was that Kevin oaf that Rory was friends with, staring right at *me*.

SECRET #25
Later can be something you dread or look forward to.
Depends what you're waiting for.

CHAPTER 26

I SURVIVED MY "LATER" with Dad.

"Ms. Sanborn told me she didn't let you stay in her room this morning and sent you out with the other students."

I nodded and could see where this conversation was headed. (*Anything happen, Timminy? Anyone give you a hard time?*) I didn't need pity and I didn't want the assistant principal part of him to take over, so I steered the conversation. "She did. It was good to see some other kids before school. Rory and I even had a long chat. Guess we lost track of time."

Dad's face twisted until it looked like a mixed-up Picasso painting. One side grinned, like he was happy his *little* boy was fitting in at his new school. The other side frowned, like he didn't believe me, or I'd said something that upset him. That side must have won out, because he cleared his throat and said, "There are other kids besides Rory to hang out with at school."

I nodded. That's one thing Dad and I agreed on.

Next, I had to figure out how to make "later" happen with Abby. After getting my teeth cleaned at our new dentist's office, doing my homework, and helping get supper ready—nachos supreme casserole, my favorite— it was eight o'clock before I had a chance to call her.

"Abby, can you talk now?"

"Sure," she said.

"Good, then hang up, and I'll call you on Skype or FaceTime."

Abby laughed. "I've never used them. I'm blind. Did you forget that again already?"

"Nope. Just 'cause you can't see me, doesn't mean I don't want to see you when we talk. Also, I don't have my own phone but I *do* have my own computer, and this way we can talk anytime we want. Can you figure it out?"

She *did* figure it out with her dad's help, fortunately, because talking with Abby turned out to be almost as good as being with her.

"So when will they let you have a phone?" Abby asked. "I've had one since fourth grade."

"Lucky you," I said.

"I'm not so sure it's luck," said Abby. "I think my parents agreed because I'm blind, and they figured it was a way to keep track of me and, hopefully, keep me safer."

"What's going on with Devon?" I asked. "I didn't even notice her crutches when we were sitting and talking at lunch."

"She has something called hereditary spastic paraplegia. Don't worry, you won't catch it—like you can't catch my blindness and I can't catch your shortness."

"Ha-ha! Not funny! I wasn't worried about catching it. Just wanted to know how she's doing."

"She's pretty cool with it," Abby said. "It is getting worse though. Someday she'll need a walker and then later a wheelchair to get around as her leg and hip muscles get weaker. But she keeps her upper body strong and hopes PT will keep her from needing more leg support for as long as possible."

"PT?" I asked.

"Physical therapy."

"Oh, I get it. My mom does speech therapy—maybe it's called ST. Now let's talk about MRD."

"MRD?" asked Abby.

"Yes, MRD—Mrs. Russell's disability."

Abby laughed. "Oh, I'm trying not to let that woman drive me crazy. She's sooooo different from the ed tech I had the last three years. Mrs. Simonds was the best and very funny, but she moved to Florida. She hated Maine winters."

I interrupted. "That doesn't explain Mrs. Russell."

"Last year she was an ed tech at the elementary school with a kindergarten girl. I think she's adjusting to the fact that I'm more independent and don't need her to hold my hand or butter my bread. She shouldn't even go to lunch with me. Mrs. Simonds never did, but Mrs. Russell says, 'I want to learn as much as I can about you, dear.'"

"Mrs. Russell does seem to have an attitude."

"Yeah," agreed Abby. "She's uncomfortable with both kid talk and blind talk, so she tries to control every conversation."

I laughed. "She should know there's no controlling us middle schoolers."

I paused. It's the first time I'd thought of *myself* as a middle school kid and didn't flinch or barf or anything.

Woof! Woof! Woof!

"Is that my favorite puppy?" asked Abby.

"Sure is. She walked in and the second she saw you on the computer screen, she started wagging her tail and barking. She knows it's you, Abby."

"Aww, Maxi, way to make me feel special. What a good girl!"

Woof! Woof! Whiiiiiiiine!

"What's she doing now?"

I laughed. "She jumped up, with her front paws on my desk. Man, she's getting tall. I think she was going to lick the computer screen. But when she got close and couldn't smell you, she got upset and started whining. She wants it to be the real you."

"Aww, Maxi, you're too cute. Now I see why we should be doing FaceTime, Timminy."

"The screen works both ways, Abby. Now I get to see your secrets, you book hoarder you."

"You mean these?" Abby asked as she ran her hand across a whole row of books.

"Yeah, those."

"It's my can't-wait-to-read stash."

"Whoa!" I said.

"I'm going to be a librarian when I grow up—"

"Really? But wouldn't that be hard since you're—"

"Blind? Yeah, it'll be a challenge, but challenges don't scare me, if you haven't noticed. You haven't seen all the special software and adaptive equipment they have for the blind. By the time I go to college, they'll have even more."

"Your books—are they *regular* books?"

"Yes, regular in that they tell the same story you read, but I read braille books sometimes, audiobooks other times, and JAWS is good too."

"The old shark movie?"

Abby laughed. "No, JAWS is a software program on PC computers that reads the words on the screen aloud to me, or VoiceOver on Macs does the same thing too."

"Cool, you'll have to show me how it works sometime."

"Sure."

"Until then, could you do me a favor?"

"Maybe?" Abby sounded suspicious.

"Don't worry—nothing that will poke out your eyeballs. Could you recommend some books for me? I haven't been reading anything other than school books lately." (Even though I'd been sitting at the reading nerd table!)

"Will do," said Abby. "Now you know my dream job, what's yours—besides being tall?"

"I don't know. I've only ever thought about what I can't be when I grow up—since I'm so short. Can't be a butcher and see over the counter or an NBA player or an air force pilot—gotta be sixty-four inches for that one. Let me think about it and get back to you."

"No rush," said Abby. She almost looked pleased.

So I asked, "Why the smile?"

Abby laughed. "I forget that you can see me with FaceTime. I'm smiling because it's nice for you not to have an answer for once. You always jump in with one of your jokes or sarcastic comments—so people can't get to know the real you."

Then she hung up.

Abby didn't give me a chance to say anything back, which was okay. For once, I had nothing to say.

But I grinned later when I saw Abby's email with the subject line: Book Recommendations for Timminy— You're Welcome! She'd put everything into a spreadsheet with titles, authors, publication dates, lists of awards they'd won, even a space to write my critique for each book. Phew! Abby was some serious about her librarian dream.

I hit reply and said, "Looks kind of like a homework assignment! Thanks, I think!"

SECRET #26
We all need dreams.

CHAPTER 27

THE NEXT MORNING I walked down the hall to meet the Beast of the East at my locker (which I think was on the south side of the building—so maybe I could be the Mouth of the South and Rory and I could become comic book characters).

But before I ever got there . . .

BAM!

Shoved inside someone else's locker!

SLAM!

Everything dark!

Just as dark as my locker, except stinkier. BO stinkier. Hadn't this kid heard about deodorant?

I jiggled the back of the lock—no luck. I didn't want to make a scene, but asphyxiation would come sooner in this locker, *much* sooner.

To scream or not to scream? That was the question. I

wasn't sure, but I thought I heard a knock a couple of lockers away, then another knock on the locker next to me, and then on the locker I was in, and then on the locker after me. Yikes, my chance to escape was escaping! So I said loud enough to be heard, but not loud enough to sound like an announcement over the intercom, "Hey! *Pssssst!* This one."

There was a pause in the knocking. Nothing happened, so I tried again, "This one here," as I knocked ever so lightly on the *inside* of the locker.

Rattle! The door opened. I gulped in fresh air, like you would before going underwater for a deep dive, in case the locker was gonna slam shut again. But it didn't, and there was . . .

My *hero*?

The Beast of the East.

He yanked me out and shut the locker.

"Your locker?" I asked.

"Nope."

"Stinks like you."

"I said nope."

"Then whose?"

"Ain't sayin'."

"One of your buddies? Got a thug to do your dirty work?"

"Shut up, Minny. You weren't at your locker so I figured it happened again. You're an easy target."

"Yeah, this is getting to be a bad habit. I really do need to learn how to jimmy open lockers."

"Then you figure it out," said Rory. "I don't share my secrets with pipsqueaks. Pipsqueaks who insult me."

He stomped off.

I slunk off.

Maybe it *was* time to shut up. I hoped that was possible, since my smart-aleck mouth seemed to have a life of its own.

At lunchtime, I headed straight to Abby's table, determined to shut my mouth. Just watch, listen, and get to know everyone better. Even if they teased me about last Friday's lunch disaster, I'd shut up. Even if Mrs. Russell started in with her she-rules-kids-drool attitude, I'd shut up. It was time to start learning how to fit in—if that was even possible.

NOT.

POSSIBLE.

I hadn't even sat down when I knew I'd never fit in.

NEVER.

There was a booster seat on the empty chair next to Abby.

A booster seat for a toddler . . . waiting for *me*.

I glared at the booster seat.

Everyone was laughing.

"So you think this is funny?" It was hard to talk between gritted teeth.

"What's funny?" asked Abby.

"No need to pull your innocent act, Ab—"

Mrs. Russell interrupted. "Timminy's wish came true already, to be taller."

Brian chuckled. "Yeah, Abby, feel beside you. There's a booster seat for Timminy."

Abby's arm reached out. When she felt the plastic booster seat, her head fell back and she clapped her hands as she squealed in delight.

I stared at each of them, even longer at Abby. I wanted to make sure she felt my stare.

"*Not* funny," I growled.

Abby and her friends stopped laughing—but it was too late.

A shout ricocheted from across the cafeteria. "HEY, WHO'S THE BABY WITH THE BOOSTER SEAT?"

I looked from this table to the next and the next. Everyone was staring, pointing, laughing . . .

At me.

Me—one big joke!

I knew they were waiting for me to say *something*.

But I held back.

At least I remembered my promise to myself. To *shut* my mouth.

I hadn't made any promises about my hands though. And they couldn't hold back the anger gushing out of me. Just like hands can't hold back a flooding river.

I picked up the booster seat, took two steps away from the table, and slammed it as hard as I could.

CRASH!

It bounced across the table, sent two lunch trays skidding to the floor, and then . . .

IT SMACKED DEVON!

Knocked her backward off her seat with her metal crutches clattering and clunking in two different directions.

Gasps replaced laughter.

I gulped down my own gasp.

A second gasp filled the cafeteria as the word *Timminy!* rang out.

Pronounced correctly, of course. My dad. No, *Mister* Harris.

Mr. Harris stared at me. Everyone stared at me—except Abby. Let them stare. All of them.

I did not care.

Take that, booster seat!

Take that, Dad!

Take that, Skenago Middle School!

SECRET #27

When the world gnaws on you day after day, there comes a day when they reach the bone and you just can't take it anymore.

CHAPTER 28

WHEN I LEFT the cafeteria, my instincts said, *Run!*
To my secret stall in the bathroom. But I didn't.

I wasn't going to hide anymore. Hiding hadn't
worked—short as I was, they still found and tortured me.

So I stood outside the cafeteria with my arms folded
and my mouth shut. Let them all gawk at me. Take pictures if they wanted. Show their friends. Enter me in the
Guinness World Records for shortest middle school loser.

Some students came up to me as they left the cafeteria. I stared straight ahead like a wax museum figure.
They moved their mouths but I didn't hear a thing. It
was as if my ears had *shut* too, along with my mouth.
For the first time, I realized how good Maxi had it. She
could shut out part of the world. I wanted to shut out
all of it.

Except for Maxi.

When Mr. Harris stepped up, I couldn't hear anything

he said either. Maybe he didn't say anything. Maybe he had locked his words inside too, for later.

I followed him. We both knew that's what he wanted.

I sat outside his office and stared straight ahead.

Mom picked me up. She knew better than to talk to me. No Maxi in the car this time.

When we got home, Maxi's tail thump-thump-thumped against the wall as she raced to greet me in the entryway. I leaned down, and she licked my face as she tried to wash away my day. But even she didn't have the power to do that.

I think I took her out to do her business. But I can't be sure. When you do something day after day, it doesn't register. Was it today or yesterday I brushed my teeth, combed my hair, took Maxi out? Some things in life work on autopilot. I could handle the autopilot parts. You don't have to feel when you're on autopilot.

We ended up in my room. On my bed. For days. Just letting each other be. No pressure. Just be.

I heard my parents talking, trying to coax me into opening up, but I kept staring at the ceiling, Maxi still at my side.

I might never be ready to talk. And I loved Maxi for being okay with that.

SECRET #28

Everyone needs somebody to let them just be.

CHAPTER 29

THE ONLY THING that mattered was Maxi. She stayed with me. She knew I wasn't ready to be alone. So she stayed.

Until Saturday. Maxi had to go to her obedience class. But she wouldn't leave me. My parents hooked her leash to her collar and tugged, but she threw a paw across my chest and wouldn't let go. They tried to lift her off my bed, but she burrowed her head under me and spread her paws out in every direction trying to dig in.

Mom sighed and said, "Timminy, can you help us with Maxi?"

I looked at Maxi and said, "She won't go unless I go."

"Then let's go!" said Mom. "We're going to be late."

I gestured with my head toward the door. No need to use words. Maxi couldn't hear and we had both figured out how to understand each other without words.

She jumped off the bed and wagged her tail like crazy.

She was excited to leave this cave we'd been hibernating in. Poor girl. Even though she looked like a polar bear, she wasn't the kind of bear that was supposed to hibernate. Her windshield-wiper tail wag turned into a full-circle, windmill tail wag. She only wagged that way when she was extra excited. I felt myself smile for the first time in days, just a little, at *her* happiness. It felt strange and good all at the same time, as if something were waking up inside me.

When we got to her class, Maxi wouldn't get out of the car unless I did.

Mom sighed and passed Maxi's leash to me. "Here, Maxi wants you, Timminy."

I wasn't sure what to do, but then I remembered Maxi knew. She'd been here before so I followed her lead. It might be a class to teach Maxi new ways of behaving, but it seemed Mom and I were the ones learning new behaviors.

Maxi's class was filled with squirming, yapping puppies in every shape and size. And their owners came in every shape and size too, but mostly they were my mom's age and they cooed over one another's puppies. I tried to ignore them. Maxi and I weren't here to socialize. We had work to do.

Things started with a review of the last lesson, practicing sit and stay. Maxi had those mastered—most of the time. The next command was down, which meant lie down on the ground. I needed to make up a sign language signal for down. Common sense was my guide. I held my arm out straight in front of me and then lowered it while saying "down." Of course, Maxi stayed up, but I looked around and saw that so did all the other puppies. The instructor walked by and whispered, "Don't forget the cheese." So the next time, I held a chunk of that stinky horseradish cheese in my hand as I lowered my arm all the way to the ground. The front half of Maxi's body lowered as if she were bowing, so then I reached back with my other hand and pushed down on her butt. It worked! Maxi lay down and got the cheese, and I got a pat on the back from the instructor. "Nice job, kid."

"Nice job, pup." I patted Maxi.

She followed the down command over and over, until I no longer had to push on her butt or say the word *down*. I just did the gesture. She understood and knew the cheese was coming her way as long as she lay down when I gestured downward with my arm. The instructor noticed and gave me a thumbs-up.

Next was the come command. All I had to do was get Maxi to sit and stay. Then I walked away from her, said "come," and made a big waving, beckoning gesture with the cheese in my hand. Maxi came bounding right to me to get the cheese.

"Hope to see you two next week," the instructor said as class ended. I smiled and nodded.

I planned on practicing the commands with Maxi every day. This next week would be all about her. She'd made the last few days all about me so it was my turn to pay her back—not that she expected it. Maxi never expected anything. She was grateful each time she got food, pats, loving. She never took them for granted.

I hoped I never took her for granted.

SECRET #29
When you expect nothing . . . everything is a treat.

CHAPTER 30

WHEN WE GOT home, my parents asked me to show them what Maxi had learned at obedience school. I said, "Later, I promise. But first, Dad, I need you to take me to see someone."

He blew out a big breath and asked, "Abby?"

"Not Abby."

"That's good," he said. "I talked to her parents and she's not ready to see you. Not yet anyway."

Dad looked at me like he expected an answer. There was no answer. I wasn't ready to see her either.

"Devon," I said. "I need to see Devon."

"Are you sure?"

I nodded.

"What if she's not ready to see you either, Timminy?"

"Then I'll do the stay command and wait outside her house until she is."

Dad drove straight to Devon's house. I didn't ask how

he knew where she lived, but probably the assistant principal part of him had already paid a visit to make sure she was all right and to talk with her parents.

"Want me to come in with you?" asked Dad.

"No, I need to do this alone."

I walked in slow motion to the front door, rubbed my sweaty palms on my jeans, and knocked.

A woman who looked like Devon answered. "May I help you?" Her voice was soft and her eyes kind.

"I'm Timminy Harris. I need to talk to Devon."

Her eyes widened, but still she reached out and shook my hand. "Nice to meet you. I'm Patrisse Willette, Devon's mom. Let me tell Devon you're here."

I wiped my palms five more times before Mrs. Willette came back and said, "Follow me."

She led me to the dining room, where Devon sat at the table drawing in a sketchbook. She closed it as I stepped closer.

I couldn't wait a second longer. "I'm sorry, Devon. Really sorry. I didn't mean to hit you."

"I know," she said, "Just like you didn't mean to drop your tray on Mrs. Russell."

What did that mean? I looked closer to try to read Devon's expression.

But then her mom interrupted. "Do you two want something to eat or drink?"

Devon didn't miss a beat. "I'll have some peanut

butter cookies and milk, but you can bring Timminy bread and water."

I leaned closer still. Was she serious? Then I saw it. The twinkle, the mischievous twinkle in her eye, and I burst out laughing. "I didn't expect that."

Devon giggled. "Why not? You should know anyone who's friends with Abby has to have a sense of humor."

I wanted to agree and say that even someone who *used to be* friends with Abby had to have a sense of humor. But that would sound like I was whining, and I was so finished with whining.

I sat down, popped a cookie in my mouth, and said, "But seriously, Devon, did I hurt you?"

She pushed up her sleeve and showed me a black-and-blue-turned-greenish-yellow bruise on her arm.

"Ouch! Sorry!" I said.

"I've had worse. If you only knew how many times I've fallen over the years."

"But still, I'm sorry. Plus I embarrassed you."

Devon said, "The opposite actually. You knocked me over like a good strike in bowling. Then I scooted one way—those cafeteria floors are slick—and grabbed one crutch, scooted the other way and grabbed my other crutch. Before anyone could help me, I was standing back up, like a reset bowling pin. Everyone said how surprised they were I got up on my own—maybe they'll stop babying me so much now."

I downed another cookie and chugged some milk. "I didn't see you get back up."

"You couldn't see anything, Timminy. Your anger was a blindfold."

I swallowed hard remembering my anger.

I was still angry—but not at Devon—I knew she wasn't the one who planted the booster seat. She really was okay and her mom wasn't having me arrested, so I did the only logical thing . . . ate another cookie.

Since Devon was braver than I'd thought, I asked, "What's in there?" as I pointed at her sketchbook.

Devon blushed. "I don't show just anyone my drawings."

"I'm not just anyone. I'm the guy who bowled you over."

Devon smiled and said, "All right," as she opened her book and then put both her hands over her face as she peeked at my reaction between her fingers.

I covered my face with my hands, too, before I shot milk snot out my nose or cookie slime out my mouth. I could hardly stop laughing.

"Man, Devon, these are great!"

"Really?"

"Really! REALLY!" I flipped through page after page, laughing so hard at Devon's cartoon drawings . . . the booster seat bowling, her own milk snot, the dumped food on Mrs. Russell . . . and so many other scenes I hadn't lived through, but they were all captured perfectly by Devon—the details, expressions, and speech bubbles of her own life's comics.

Devon blushed and said, "Thanks."

I clinked my milk glass with hers . . .

"A toast to you, Devon!"

SECRET #30
Everyone has hidden talents.

CHAPTER 31

IF DEVON COULD face middle school every day, I figured I could too. No more running away. Let the bullies do what they would.

I told my parents some of my new school rules. "When I go back Monday, I'm riding the bus instead of going with you, Dad. I'll check with each of my teachers to make up what I've missed. Is there anyone else I need to apologize to besides Devon?"

My parents looked at each other, baffled.

So I said, "Talk about it, and let me know," and went to my room.

I'd apologize to anyone Dad wanted me to, except Abby. I had thought she was a true friend. Everyone else could laugh about the booster seat, but not Abby. She knew better. It would be like me laughing at her because she's blind. I'd been wrong about Abby. But now I knew the REAL ABBY.

On Monday morning, I had to flag down the bus, since the driver wasn't used to stopping for me. I sat in the first open seat, in the fourth row. I didn't realize all the elementary students sat up front.

Rory got on the bus right after me. As he walked by, to the back of the bus, I waited for him to say something, but he didn't. He ignored me. As well as a couple of the loudmouth elementary kids.

"Bigfoot's back!"

"Jolly Green Giant!"

"He's not jolly—he's crabby."

I shook my head. Man, does bullying start as soon as babies learn to talk? I was surprised that all Rory did was let out a loud sigh.

But Rory's friend Kevin didn't ignore anyone. He swaggered onto the bus and when a kid said, "Another bigfoot," Kevin said, "Shut up, squirt, or I'll squish you."

The bus driver shouted, "Sit down, Kevin, unless you want me to report you to the office again."

Kevin said, "Go ahead." Then he stopped in front of me and smirked—like I'd made his day by riding on the bus. Then he walked toward the back.

As the rest of the bus filled, I heard the buzz from the other middle schoolers.

"That's *him*!"

"Booster-seat baby!"

"Smacked that poor girl with the crutches."

"Who's he think he is?"

"Bet his assistant principal daddy said, 'Dat's aw-wight, my witto boy.'"

I jerked my head around, ready to yell "Shut up." They could pick on me, but leave my dad out of this. I saw Kevin in one backseat laughing and Rory in the other backseat staring straight ahead. That reminded me of my new plan—let the bullies do what they will. I *wouldn't* talk.

I mostly kept my no-talk pledge the rest of the day except when I walked past Abby's table in the cafeteria. Devon smiled at me, so I said hi.

She said, "Glad you're back, Timminy." Becca and Brian waved too. Abby scowled and said something under her breath, which made Mrs. Russell pat her on the hand.

I headed to my old "reading" table. The two guys looked up from their books, then went right back to reading. I could hear the buzz starting . . .

"He's baaaack!"

"Wonder what he'll throw today."

"Get ready to duck."

"Good thing pipsqueaks don't have much strength."

Since I wasn't going to say anything, there was no reason to listen to them.

I stuck my nose in the book I'd brought. Abby might not be my friend anymore, but she *did* know books. I'd checked her list over the weekend and saw that I had one of the books she recommended on my bookshelf, about a dog called Shiloh. I read half over the weekend and kept reading at lunch. Maxi wasn't with me, but it was still nice having a fictional dog for company. Beagles are kind of cute, but nothing compared to a Pyr who is Pyr-fect. I smiled at my joke as I kept reading and rooting for Shiloh.

I *was* able to tune out all the talk around me that day, and the rest of the week too. That was my goal—to make all my time at school go by quickly—and then switch it so that all my time with Maxi went in slo-o-o-o-w mo-o-o-o-otion.

I'd found out what I had to make up in all my classes. So that's what Maxi and I did every day after school—my homework and her homework. Sit, stay, down, come—she was getting trained. Shut up, don't react to others, read—I was getting trained too.

SECRET #31
It's never too late to learn new tricks.

CHAPTER 32

IT WAS SATURDAY, time for Maxi to learn new commands. Mom agreed I would be Maxi's teacher at obedience class again.

We spent most of the class reviewing old lessons. Puppies need lots of repetition to learn—especially *deaf* puppies. Finally, the instructor showed us a new command: shake, for shaking paws.

The only thing I shook was my head as I looked the instructor right in the eye and said, "I'm not teaching Maxi shake. She's a deaf dog. Shaking paws won't keep her safe. It's just a show-off trick."

The instructor grinned and said in a low voice, "You're right. It doesn't make sense for Maxi, but most dog owners love the shake trick. Why don't you two step over to the side and I'll show you a different command."

I led Maxi to the side where the instructor showed us the "leave it" command, which meant to leave something alone—like porcupines! I came up with a sign for the command—a karate-chop action with my hand moving between Maxi and whatever I wanted her to leave. We used a ball as the object for Maxi to leave, but whenever I put my hand between Maxi and the ball and did the "leave it" sign, she just licked my hand. It smelled like cheese. The instructor grinned and said, "Keep practicing."

When Maxi and I jumped into the car and I told Mom I'd refused to teach Maxi the trick of the day, she stared at me in the rearview mirror and kicked up the volume on her voice. "But, Timminy, Maxi needs to learn everything she can. Your father and I feel it would be best if . . ."

Then she stopped, shook her head, and said, "You know what's best for Maxi, so focus on what *you* think she needs to learn. Who am I to argue?"

I scrunched my eyebrows and gave her an are-you-sure? look back in the mirror. She laughed. "I know, you're thinking someone kidnapped your bossy mother and left some wimp in her place. Don't worry. I can still give orders if I need to. But on this, I trust you."

"Really?"

"Really, Timminy."

"Thanks, Mom. I won't let you down."

Mom's eyes smiled in the mirror. "I know you won't let me or Maxi down."

● ● ●

When we got home, I got back to work teaching Maxi the leave-it command. We kept practicing and practicing. It was hard, but she was starting to understand, except I didn't know what to do when she wasn't looking at me. I needed her to learn to leave things she was going after if I wasn't right next to her.

"How's it going?" Dad asked when he came out to check on us.

I sighed. "She's getting better when she's looking at me and paying attention, but when she's busy in her own puppy world, forget it. I may as well be giving commands to that rock over there."

Dad smiled. "Maybe we can cast a spell on Maxi to make her look at you."

"Dad! That's it!" I gave him a hug.

He looked confused.

"Just stay with Maxi," I said, adding the sign for stay, before racing upstairs to my computer.

I found the pages I'd bookmarked, printed them out, raced back downstairs, grabbed Mom by the hand, and said, "Come on! I've got something to show you and Dad."

When we got outside, Maxi was sleeping and Dad was dozing in a lawn chair. I shook him. "Wake up, Dad. I figured out how we can get Maxi to look at us."

My parents waited.

"A pager collar," I said. "The collar goes on Maxi and then one of us holds the control switch to it. When we turn it on, her collar vibrates—it *pages* her—so she knows we're talking to her. We train her to look at us, see our sign language command, and follow it. They cost around three hundred dollars, depending on the model you get."

I held out the pages I'd printed. "Here are all the details."

"Wow, you've done your research," Mom said. "Timminy, order the best one for Maxi. And, Kenneth, cough up your credit card." Dad rolled his eyes at Mom's command. I grinned. It was nice to have the Boss back when she was rooting for me . . . and Maxi.

Dad and I placed the order. We were told to expect delivery within five to ten business days—that meant it could be here this coming week! Maxi yipped in her sleep—a yip of approval, I hoped.

As she slept, I did more research, since I was on a roll. Not pager collars—we had that figured out. But MIRA, the organization for the blind that gave younger kids guide dogs. I knew Abby and I might never be friends again, but she still should know about MIRA. I wasn't going to tell her face-to-face as I'd originally planned so I could see one of her whole-face-lights-up smiles. Nope, I didn't care if I ever saw Abby smile again. I'd seen her scowl—the real Abby. But keeping what I'd learned from her would be cruel, and I refused to be cruel like some other people I knew. So I sent her an email with links to what I'd discovered.

Not that I was checking, but whenever I went online the rest of the weekend, I saw there was no reply from Abby. Not even a simple thanks.

SECRET #32
You don't need a thanks to know you've done the right thing.

CHAPTER 33

AFTER SURVIVING LAST week at school, I relaxed a little. It was still my least favorite place to be, but I'd figured I could get through each day till it was time to get home to Maxi. And that's all that mattered.

My lunch survival plan stayed the same. Eat, read, ignore.

I was already on my third book from Abby's list after visiting the school library. *Shiloh* went back on my shelf, *Winn-Dixie* had been a winner, and now *Marley* was the best *worst* dog I'd ever met. He made Maxi look like a saint. I was trying to eat a taco one-handed at the same time I was turning the pages and trying not to laugh out loud at Marley's thunderstorm-wreck-the-house panic attacks when I heard a clicking sound that was too quiet and rhythmic for the thunder sound effects playing out in my head.

I looked up. *Click-click*—Devon's crutches. Next to

her was Abby being led by Brian, then Becca, everyone, except for Mrs. Russell. I turned and saw Mrs. Russell standing at their usual table with her hands on her hips and a scowl on her face.

"Mind if we join you?" Devon asked as she stood directly behind me.

I didn't answer.

"Join who?" asked Abby. "You guys said our table was taken today. Whose table is this?"

I still didn't answer, but someone else did.

"Hurry up and sit down. Can't you see we're trying to read?" said the redhead boy at my table. It's the first time I'd ever heard his voice.

Abby looked confused, but sat in an empty seat where Brian had led her, and Becca sat down too, but Devon still stood directly behind me. My instincts were to bolt. But if I did, I'd knock Devon over. Even I wouldn't do that again.

I went back to my book and tried to ignore them.

But I should have known the word *read* would get Abby talking. "So who are you and what are you reading?"

"I'm Carver, and I'm reading *The Westing Game*," said the redhead.

"And I'm Benjamin, reading *Hoot*," said the other one.

They both looked at me. When I didn't say anything, Benjamin said, "And that's Timminy Harris."

Carver added, "And he's reading *Marley & Me*."

"WHAT?!" Abby and I shouted at the same time.

"Keep it down," warned the teacher on duty as she walked by.

"How'd you know who I was?" I whisper-shouted at the two reading nerds.

"Everyone knows who you are," said Carver.

Of course, even their stacks of books weren't big enough barriers to barricade them from me and my booster-seat tirade. Poor guys. They'd been stuck at the same table with the wild, crazy, short kid.

"I'm not sitting at the same table with him," Abby whisper-shouted as she stood up.

Click-click. Devon moved behind Abby and said, "Oh yes, you are."

"No way," said Abby. "Timminy hurt you. I can't forgive him."

"He didn't mean to," said Devon. "He's already apologized, and I've forgiven him, so get over it, Abby."

Devon wasn't behind me anymore, so I stood up. "Good try, Devon. But *I'm* the one who's never forgiving Abby."

Click-click. Devon started moving back toward me, but then she stopped and shout-shouted, "STOP IT, BOTH OF YOU! OR I'LL HIT YOU WITH MY CRUTCHES, AND DON'T THINK I WON'T!"

"*Sit, Devon!*" Abby and I both whisper-shouted

before Devon realized what she'd done and died of embarrassment.

Devon sat.

Brian started, "The booster seat—we didn't know—"

"Oh, you knew all right," I interrupted. "When I got to the table you were all grinning at how funny you thought you were. I know what I saw."

"Wait!" Devon gasped. "You thought *we* put the booster seat there?"

Becca jumped in, "The booster seat was already there when we sat down, in the place you'd sat the day before. We thought it was *you* who'd put it there. As a joke. And to be honest, we thought it was funny."

I shook my head. "That's crazy. Why would I bring a booster seat to lunch?"

"AS A JOKE!" Devon said. She was really getting into this shouting.

"Why would I joke about being short?" I wasn't buying their crazy explanation.

Abby finally spoke. "Timminy, you joke about being short all the time!"

Brian agreed. "Yeah, when Mrs. Russell asked what you wanted to be when you grew up, you said—"

"TALL!" everyone shouted.

"Yeah," Devon said. "I was impressed how you could laugh at yourself. I wish I could—I didn't even dare to admit I was the milk snorter."

"You, Devon, really?" asked Abby.

Devon blushed—she still couldn't laugh at her own milk snorting.

"Wait," I said. "If what you say is true, then *who* put the booster seat there?"

"Shouldn't you know?" asked Carver. "Don't you keep track of your enemies?"

I looked at Carver. The mystery-reading book boy had a point.

Brrrrng. Lunch was over. I wasn't sure whether I was glad or not. I looked at my lunch tray and saw my abandoned taco. Oh, well, Maxi and I would have to have a bigger after-school snack.

I stood up and said, "I'll try to forgive and forget, and I'll sit at your lunch table tomorrow if you'll help me figure out who planted the booster seat."

"I'll help," said Carver.

"And me too?" asked Benjamin.

"Sure! You both can," Abby said with a smile, even though she couldn't have seen the rest of us already nodding. "It means there won't be enough room for Mrs. Russell though. Too bad."

As we were leaving, Abby said, "Timminy, before you go . . . I'm not sure I'm ready to forgive you yet for what you did to Devon. But now that I know it wasn't on purpose, and that you really thought we did the booster seat, and . . ."

"And what, Abby?"

"And thanks for the email you sent. Thanks—that's all."

And that was enough—for now.

SECRET #33
When you're stubborn, it takes longer to get over a misunderstanding.

CHAPTER 34

AS SOON AS I got home from school, I saw an email from Abby: *Wanna come over and talk MIRA?*

I put Maxi on her leash and we headed over.

Abby's screams hurt my ears. "MIRA! YAAAAAA-AAAY! MY CHANCE FOR A GUIDE DOG!"

Thank goodness Maxi was deaf. She couldn't hear Abby's screaming, but she saw her excitement, and joined in. *WOOF! YAP! HOWL!*

Maxi jumped up on Abby, and they did a happy dance.

I just watched and laughed.

When they stopped, I pulled a rawhide treat and a box of graham crackers out of my backpack and Abby got us some peanut butter to spread on the crackers. She even spread some on Maxi's treat. Then we all chowed down.

"That's enough," Abby said, pushing away the crackers.

She sucked in a deep breath and said, "Do you think MIRA is real or a mirage?"

"A minute ago you were cheering, Abby, and now you're a skeptic."

"I can't help it. I've been waiting so long. What do you think—real or mirage?"

"Real, Abby. I wouldn't have shared it with you if I didn't think it was a real possibility for you."

Abby's face glowed. It was good to see her away from school without her dark glasses. "I'm not sure why they'd let younger blind kids—as young as me—have guide dogs when all the other places make us wait until we're sixteen."

"Maybe they know kids like you are ready, have been ready for a long time."

"But North Carolina is so far away from Maine, to go for training."

"It's not the moon," I said.

"How'd I miss MIRA all the times I searched for guide dog options?"

"Maybe 'cause it started in Canada and is new in the US. Plus all the other places said you were too young so you believed them and stopped looking."

"What if I am too young?"

"You don't believe that."

As Abby and I batted words back and forth, Maxi

moved her head from my lap to Abby's lap as if she were really listening to us.

"What if my parents say no?" asked Abby.

"What if they say yes?"

"Even if they say yes, what are the odds MIRA will choose me to get a dog? They must have so many blind kids wanting dogs. I couldn't stand it if they said no."

"Abby, if you don't try MIRA, then you won't have a guide dog until you're sixteen. So then it's already a no. But if you try MIRA, you have a chance for one now, a maybe."

Abby let out the longest sigh. "See, that's why I had to talk to you before my parents. If I don't believe this will work and can't answer their questions, there's no way I'll convince them. There are so many reasons why it shouldn't work . . . How could a dog from North Carolina adjust to Maine winters? Blind kids in the city must need guide dogs more than blind kids out in the country—they have so many more obstacles. Getting a dog from MIRA is free, that's good, but dogs still cost a lot and I don't have a job to help pay for . . ."

Maxi started to snore. Smart girl. I'd had enough too.

"Stop!" I shouted.

Abby's lips quivered a bit, but she did stop talking.

"Good," I said. "Before you make any more excuses why you won't get a dog from MIRA, remember what you told me once: *Challenges don't scare me.*"

Abby smiled.

I waited.

She kept smiling.

"Sooooo?" I said.

"I don't have anything to say. You're right—they don't."

And that was that. Abby stopped making excuses.

"So when you gonna tell your parents?" I asked.

"Tonight at supper."

"Want some moral support?"

"Are you inviting yourself for one of my mom's fancy SpaghettiOs dinners?"

"Um, I think I still have some graham crackers left."

"Never mind, you're not invited anyway. I'm up for this challenge . . . alone. But thanks."

Sleeping Maxi suddenly started wagging her tail—maybe because she was dreaming about SpaghettiOs with meatballs or maybe it was her way of clapping her approval to Abby. *Whop-whop-whop.*

SECRET #34
Sometimes you have to be talked into wanting something you already wanted.

CHAPTER 35

AT LUNCH THE next day, we hatched a plan to figure out who was the booster-seat bandit.

"Do you think the same person who planted the booster seat also shoved you in lockers?" asked Carver.

I nodded. "Probably."

"Any suspects?" asked Carver.

I grinned at how serious he was taking all this. "Rory is suspect number one."

"But I thought he let you out of lockers," said Abby.

"He did, but maybe he did that to throw me off his trail."

"Anyone else?" continued Carver.

"Rory's buddy Kevin might have done it. Or maybe Kevin and Rory were working together."

Abby jumped in. "I heard Kevin's mom has a new live-in boyfriend with a toddler. Toddlers use booster seats. Maybe he snatched it away from the little guy and brought it to school—"

"For me, another little guy." I finished her sentence.

Abby laughed. Everyone else at our table looked at her as if they were wondering if it was okay to laugh. I couldn't help it—I laughed at Abby's laugh and suddenly the whole table was cracking up, except Carver.

He cleared his throat and said, "Back to business. Just those two suspects, Timminy?"

I paused. "No, it could also be the guys who shove me around in the hall and in the cafeteria."

"Boy, you have a lot of enemies for a new kid," said Carver. "But don't worry—we'll figure it out. Tomorrow morning we'll all be spies."

I chuckled at Carver, the spymaster.

But I wasn't chuckling the next morning, when his plan to use me as bait actually worked.

SLAM!

I was shoved inside a locker. Hooray! I gave a little fist pump.

It was my own locker this time and not so stinky. The homeroom bell had rung and I'd lingered as long as I could in front of my open locker—hoping that would lure the bully. It did!

But when I didn't hear any rescuers coming, I got worried . . . Uh-oh! Maybe I'd stayed after the homeroom bell a little too long and none of my spies had. Were they already in homeroom thinking our plan had failed for today? Had they all left the scene of the crime before the crime?

But then I heard whispering.

It was Carver. "Hey, Timminy, we got our guy."

"Good. Don't let him escape," I said.

"The others are following him. They told me to stay here with you."

"Great, so let me out."

"What's your combination?"

I told him, heard the dial turning, and waited for the locker to open. It didn't.

"Come on, Carver."

"Sorry, Timminy, I'm a fifth grader too, and it takes me a few tries to open my *own* locker."

I half laughed and sighed at the same time. I could identify with Carver. I heard the dial turning again . . . and again . . . and . . .

"Move outta the way, kid!" A deeper voice.

RATTLE!

My locker door flew open.

Carver was staring up in awe at the Beast of the East.

"It's you!" I yelled at Rory. "You're the bad guy!"

Carver looked nervous. "No, he's not the bad guy."

"He's *not*?"

Rory folded his arms, looking from Carver to me, and

back again. "Who you calling a bad guy, Minny? The guy who keeps saving you? Bet I could fit both of you in this locker."

Before I could yell to Carver to "RUN FOR YOUR LIFE," I saw Abby and everyone else walking down the hall toward us, including my dad.

Mister Harris took charge.

"What's going on here?"

"Um . . . er . . ." I looked at the others.

Rory jumped in. "Mr. AP, let me explain."

Dad interrupted him. "Wait, Rory. I want to hear your side. But I want to talk with each of you *alone*. So, please, all follow me and wait outside my office for your turn."

Carver looked like he was gonna puke. I doubted the book kid had ever even seen the inside of an assistant principal's office. Being a spy was much safer in a book than out in the real world. So I spoke up, "Dad, um . . . Mr. Harris, Carver here was walking by. You didn't see anything. Did you, Carver?" I shook my head no to remind Carver that he really *didn't* see anything.

"Is that true?" asked my dad.

Carver just shook, his head and his body.

"Okay, I'll give you a pass for homeroom. But I don't want to see you late for homeroom again. Do you understand?"

This time Carver tried to nod his head yes, but his whole body, head to toe, was still shaking.

Dad was one smart AP—he probably figured the answers he'd get from Carver weren't worth it. His office had carpeting and the puke smell would linger *forever*!

The rest of us followed Dad with Rory and me in the rear. Rory slowed until the others were a little ahead and whispered, "If your dad asks who put you in the locker, it was *me*. I did it."

I whispered back. "But Carver said it wasn't you. Carver's not the kind of kid to lie."

"But you lied and told your dad Carver didn't see anything. You get to protect your kind, I get to protect mine."

"Step it up." Dad turned and motioned to Rory and me.

"Yes, sir, Mr. AP."

Dad took us into his office one at a time. He kept a poker face and didn't let on what any of the others had said to him. I guess he was cut out for this assistant principal job after all.

Later, at lunch, we tried to put all our separate pieces together.

"What did you say?"

"What did he say?"

"Anyone get detention?"

"Anyone puke?"

In the end, everyone agreed it was Kevin Cole who'd shoved me into my locker. "We saw him," said Brian.

"He rushed off afterward and probably thought he'd get away with it."

"I should have known," I said.

Kevin was sitting at a table in the back of the cafeteria, staring, glaring at *our* table.

"Don't look at him!" Carver started to shake again. "He could eat us for lunch."

"Don't worry, Carver. He's after me. Maybe I teed him off the time I told him to wear a bib."

Carver shook his head in disbelief as he still quivered.

It looked like we'd solved the mystery. But as we headed to our classes after lunch, I couldn't stop thinking about one more question: Why would Rory say he was the one who shoved me in my locker when it was really Kevin? Maybe Rory had already given me the answer to that when he'd said "protect your own kind."

And who was the real Rory? Big Jerk bully—or just another middle school kid like me? Had he really been rescuing me all those times?

I put the mysteries behind me when I got home after school to focus on Maxi.

When I took her out to do her business, I took her off her leash. She'd been doing better following commands. I wanted to see if she'd hang close. Plus soon she'd be off her leash more with her pager collar arriving any day now!

Maxi was sniffing, then stopped to roll over and

wiggle on her back in the grass. Like she was trying to scratch an itch she couldn't reach. She looked silly. I laughed and then . . .

WHOMP!

Something hit one of the sliding glass doors and bounced back.

It was a small bird—some kind of sparrow, I think. The bird landed on the ground right next to Maxi. Yikes! It would only take one gulp and bye-bye, birdie.

The bird didn't move. I knew Maxi didn't hear the *whomp*. I stepped slowly toward them, hoping to rescue the bird—dead or alive—before Maxi found it. Or if Maxi looked at me, I could try the "leave it" command.

Instead, Maxi finished rolling over from her back to her stomach and—*voilà!* The bird was right by her snout. I froze. I didn't want her to think this feathery blob was one of the fuzzy tennis balls we played fetch with. (Actually, she didn't really know how to play fetch. She played keep.)

Maxi sniffed the bird. It didn't move. I took a step closer, ready to dive and rescue it if Maxi opened her mouth.

But she didn't. She sniffed it again. And then gently, ever so gently, nudged it with her snout. It still didn't move. So next she placed a paw on either side of it as if she were holding an egg she didn't want to break. The bird stirred, just a little. I jumped, but Maxi didn't. She nudged it again with her snout and then rested her head on top of it. But I could see her head was barely touching the bird, like she was trying to cover it up, keep it warm. She held that position. I held my breath. She stayed there as if she were the mother of this little creature. My heart sank—how could I break it to her that her newly adopted kid was almost dead, if not already dead?

But it was Maxi who had news for me.

She lifted her head, nudged the bird one more time with her snout, and, *whoosh*, it flew off. Just like that.

I was a little sad for Maxi, not as sad as if the bird really were dead, but still . . . she'd made a new friend and had lost it already.

Maxi didn't seem to mind. She jumped up, ran over to the tree where the bird had landed, and barked. The bird flew off the tree and in a loop over Maxi's head as if to say, "Thanks, bye, see you later."

And who knows, maybe they'd made a playdate.

SECRET #35
You never know who your own kind is.

CHAPTER 36

FINALLY, THE PAGER collar came!

THE PAGER COLLAR CAME!

I wanted to ride Maxi through the streets of Skenago like Paul Revere's horse and announce the collar's arrival. Instead, Maxi gave the FedEx driver who brought the package a kiss. And when I told him what was inside, he said, "Oh, I'm so happy for you," and he leaned down to kiss her back.

I started training Maxi the second I opened the package. At first, Maxi acted surprised when her collar vibrated. She looked in every direction as if she were on the lookout for danger or wondered whether she'd done something to trigger the vibration. But then she'd see me and wag her tail as if to say, "Ha! Ha! It's you!"

Once she'd look at me, I'd do the come sign and she'd come and I'd give her a treat. She wanted to hang around for another treat, but I'd walk off and she'd get interested in Smell #376 or Smell #842 in the universe. Then I'd trigger the collar again, she'd look at me, I'd do the come sign, and she did! For the treat!

Next, I mixed it up with the sit and stay signs, and I would bring the treat to her if she *did* sit or stay. She was confused and thought she'd only get the treat if she came to me, but that's okay. "We've only just begun, Maxi. You don't have to learn everything the first day." My parents were impressed with the collar and Maxi when they got home.

Abby was impressed, too, when I told her. She liked that Maxi would have more freedom with the collar (like she'd have more freedom once she got a guide dog). She made me promise to bring Maxi over soon and said, "I have my own new trick to show off, too, but it doesn't involve a collar." She laughed.

After school Friday, I brought Maxi over to Abby's so they could both show off. Plus Abby had promised us pizza and a movie.

But when we arrived, Abby didn't answer the door. So I opened it and hollered for her, but no answer.

Suddenly I heard Abby yelling . . .

"HEY! HEY! HEEEEEEEEEY!"

Where *was* she?

The yelling was coming from out back, past Abby's pool, toward the woods.

"YOO-HOO! WHERE ARE YOU TWO?"

I yelled back, "ABBY, I CAN HEAR YOU. MAXI CAN'T. WHERE ARE *YOU*?"

"FOLLOW MY VOICE!"

I tried, but I wasn't very good. Maxi, on the other hand, used her secret weapon, her *sniffer*!

Abby didn't say anything else to make it easier to find her. But Maxi seemed to be on Abby's scent, so I just held her leash and followed.

YIP! YAP-YAP! Maxi found Abby and leaned in to give her one of her hugs.

"Boo, you two!" said Abby, hugging Maxi back.

"What are you doing?" I asked. "You shouldn't be out in these woods alone."

"Oh, Timminy, this is my new trick, and stop babying me like Mrs. Russell does. I love these woods. I've been practicing ever since that day I walked in the woods alone at your house. I go a little farther every day. When—if—MIRA visits to figure out where I need a guide dog to lead me, I'll show them these woods."

"Yeah, but you should wait until you get the dog and *not* be out here alone, even with your cane. You're braver or crazier than I am, Abby. Which?"

"Maybe both," she said. "Not sure there's much difference between the two—and don't worry, I always have my phone with me." Abby pulled it from her pocket. "But come on, you two. We have some pizza and a movie to get to."

She started back toward her house. I *think* it was toward her house. It didn't seem like the way Maxi and I had just come. Maybe she knew a more direct path back. As I tried to figure out where we were, I realized Abby was already out of sight.

How could a blind girl walk through the woods faster than me? Short legs! Must be my *short* legs.

I didn't like the idea of Abby walking alone, so I released Maxi and said, "Go help Abby, girl." Maxi sprinted off and I followed.

But now I couldn't hear Maxi or Abby. I stopped and strained to listen. Were they standing still and trying to trick me? I took a few more steps, stopped, and listened again. I *still* didn't hear them, but the wind was blowing and fall leaves were raining down. *Crinkle* sounds were everywhere, but which sounds were Abby and Maxi?

I turned back the way I thought Maxi and I had come, walked a ways. Still no luck.

I thought about pushing the controller on Maxi's pager collar so she'd come look for me. But I didn't want her to leave Abby. Instead, I took a deep breath and yelled, "HEY! SLOW DOWN! WHERE ARE YOU? IT'S NOT FUNNY! ABBY!" My words seemed to get blown away by the wind.

Darn! Why do trees have to look alike—covered in bark and leaves? If I got lost in Portland, at least, there'd be street signs to help me figure out where I was.

I stopped walking. Was I really lost? I'd been worried about Abby and now *I* was the one in trouble. What should I do? Before I could answer my own question, I heard a familiar sound . . .

Vroom-vroom-vroom!

I headed *toward* the sound and soon found the wide trail in the woods, which made me feel better. Then I saw Rory on his ATV and I hate to admit it—that made me feel even better.

I flagged him down, and he squealed to a stop.

I thought about telling him Abby was lost in the woods and asking if he'd help me find her. But I swallowed my pride and said, "I'm lost. Do you only rescue kids from lockers?"

Rory gave a snorting laugh. I took that as a hopeful sign. "Climb on," he said. I sat behind him, trying hard not to touch him, but man, he was big and took up so much space. Plus he revved the engine as he took off. I lost my balance and almost fell off the back, so I did what anyone would do in the same situation—I put my arms around his waist and held on tight.

I shouted, "NOT MY HOUSE, ABBY'S."

He must've heard because we *vroomed* through the woods and in no time screeched to a stop at Abby's.

And there stood Abby and Maxi. I climbed off, and Maxi ran right past me, jumped up on Rory, and started licking him.

"Hey, Little Beast, that tickles," Rory said to her. "Haven't seen you since your run-in with the porcupine. How ya doing? Hope my ATV didn't scare you just now."

I said, "Maxi's deaf. She can't hear your ATV."

"Really?" asked Rory. "Poor Little Beast." He gave Maxi some extra pats. "I'll keep my eyes out for her."

"Thanks," I said. "For the ride too."

But before Rory could roar away, Abby jumped in, "We're having a pizza-movie party. Wanna join us?"

Maxi jumped back up on Rory and *woof-woof*ed her approval.

Rory looked from Abby to Maxi to me, climbed off his ATV, and said, "Sure, Ab-B-B-B. What the heck."

Rory and I must be soul brothers or something 'cause that's exactly what I was thinking . . . WHAT THE HECK?!

SECRET #36
To get through life, sometimes you have to hold on tight.

CHAPTER 37

SKENAGO.

Funny how this strange town with its strange name didn't seem quite so strange anymore. Since it was a *new* place, I could try new things.

Like watching a movie with my eyes closed.

"Abby, how the heck do you know what's going on when the actors aren't talking?"

She laughed. "Wanna know my secret, Timminy?"

Rory answered instead. "Just tell him to shut up and open his eyes so I can watch without all this talking."

Abby said, "No, you pipe down, Rory, and eat more pizza. We know that's the real reason you came over." Rory didn't argue and grabbed two more slices of pizza, one in each hand, and chowed down, taking a bite from one slice, then the other, back and forth.

"The background music gives away some of what's

happening, but my real secret . . ." Abby paused for effect.

"Yes?" I said.

"I'm not sure I should be sharing my secrets with you."

I grabbed her cane and said, "You won't get your cane back until you do."

She hugged Maxi, who was lying beside her, and said, "Then I'll use Maxi as my guide dog until I get my own dog."

Rory shouted, "You're getting a guide dog, Abby? When? Why didn't you tell me?"

"Calm down." Abby laughed. "I was going to tell you later—I thought you didn't want to interrupt the movie."

"The movie can wait," said Rory, pushing the pause button.

"What about Abby's movie-watching secret?" I asked.

Rory pointed the remote toward me as if he were pausing me too, and said, "Her secret can wait too. Guide dog can't wait. Now, Abby! Spill your guts."

Abby and I laughed at Rory, who then sat stone still as we told him all about MIRA. Abby explained that she hadn't applied for a dog yet, but her parents said she could soon. Although, there were no guarantees she'd get one.

Then she showed Rory the MIRA website on her laptop.

"Aww, Ab-B-B-B!" Rory said.

"What are you aww-ing about?" asked Abby.

"Those dogs, Abby. They're wicked cute."

"Cute like what?" asked Abby.

Rory scratched his head. "Cute like cute dogs, Abby."

Abby turned her head toward me.

I knew what she needed—blind talk—so I said, "They're Labernese, a mix of Bernese Mountain Dogs and Labs, and they look like a sideways dark-chocolate whoopie pie with extra creamy filling oozing out the middle."

"Oooh! That sounds wicked yummy," said Abby.

"Wicked!" I agreed, trying to sound more like Abby, the hard-core Mainer.

"Speaking of yummy," said Rory. "Any more pizza?"

"You're a bottomless pit, Rory." Abby chuckled.

We went back to the pizza and movie, and I finally got Abby to spill her movie-watching secret.

"I only watch movies that I've read as books first so I already know the story—although the movie is never as good as the book," she admitted.

I hadn't read the book for this movie so I watched the rest with my eyes open, while Rory ate the rest of the pizza with his mouth open—gotta teach that beast some manners!

Afterward, Rory asked, "Do you and Maxi want a ride home?"

"Nah. We'll walk."

"Ya better start wearing orange vests—Maxi too—if you go for walks. Hunting season is starting."

I glared at Abby. "Did you hear that, Abby Winslow?"

"Don't worry—I won't walk in the woods during hunting season no matter what color I'm wearing."

"Good! I don't want to find you out in the woods again *alone*," I said.

Rory rolled his eyes and muttered, "He's kinda short to be acting like your parent, Abby."

She giggled.

I ignored them and started home with Maxi—down the road, not through the woods.

I glanced down. Maxi was limping a little. Maybe she'd hurt her paw in the woods earlier. Or maybe it was stiff from lying on it through the movie—my leg had fallen asleep for a while. Or maybe Rory was right. I was a worrywart parent after all.

SECRET #37
You only worry about what you care about.

CHAPTER 38

MIRA, MIRA, on the wall, who's the fairest of them all?

Hopefully, Abby!

Not the fairest, but the *neediest* for a guide dog.

I couldn't believe she'd heard back from MIRA a week after applying. They were going to visit Abby next Wednesday, spend the day shadowing her at school and at home, plus interview the important people in her life.

Abby said, "That includes best friends. Will you talk to them, Timminy?"

"Of course," I agreed. (Was Abby saying I was her best friend? Probably not since she said *friends*—plural. But at least I was still in the running.)

At last, Wednesday arrived and so did Abby's MIRA person, Mrs. Myers. She asked a few questions, but mostly watched closely, *very* closely. We could have used her help when we were trying to capture the Booster Seat and Locker Bandit. She sat with us at our lunch table, shadowed Abby in all her classes, even followed her into the restroom.

Talk.

About.

Awkward.

She interviewed the principal, plus my dad, the librarian, even Rory. She also interviewed Abby's ed tech, Mrs. Russell, who had pages of notes. But then Mrs. Myers only talked to her for five minutes. Abby said Mrs. Russell seemed huffy afterward (maybe she was worried she'd lose her job to a four-legged creature).

Mrs. Myers visited Abby's house before school to see how she got ready and then my house after school since Abby spent so much time there. She watched Abby interact with Maxi. By her smile, I could tell Mrs. Myers thought Maxi was cute. But then she shook her head as Maxi twisted and turned trying to fit and sit on Abby's lap, and I could tell she knew Maxi was *not* guide dog material. (That was okay 'cause she was my dog material.)

Mrs. Myers wanted Abby to show her where she went and what she did outside. Even though we let her borrow an orange vest, we agreed they shouldn't go into the woods during hunting season. But Abby was honest and told Mrs. Myers she needed a guide dog to help her walk in the woods—it was the place she "felt most free." She even confessed to sometimes walking in the woods alone.

Mrs. Myers ended her day by going back to Abby's house for supper and watching her do homework on the computer. I'd offered to steal their can opener ahead of time so Abby's mom wouldn't make a SpaghettiOs supper for Mrs. Myers, but Abby said her dad was going to order pizza.

Abby called me on FaceTime after Mrs. Myers left. She looked tired, but pleased. "It's over. Mrs. Myers said she would be in touch within two weeks with an answer. More waiting."

"Promise to let me know the minute you find out."

Abby smiled. "Oh, I'll let you know all right. If it's a no, you'd better get ear protectors because I won't stop screaming, 'NO! NO! Oh NO!' If it's a yes, I've already figured out how to tell you."

"How?" I asked.

"You'll see. No one else might, but *you* will."

Abby was right. The day she found out, I walked into school, saw her, and I did know.

"Yes! YES! Oh YES!" I shouted as I ran up to Abby in the hallway. I tried to lift her and twirl her around to celebrate. In that moment, I forgot I was small, but I still managed to lift Abby an inch or two off the floor as we both laughed and shouted, "Yes! YES! Oh YES!"

Everyone gathered around us.

"What's going on?"

"Why are you two shouting?"

"What's all this YESSING about?"

I was bursting to shout the answer, but it was Abby's news to tell, not mine.

She decided to toy with everyone and stretch out her news. "What makes you think anything's going on? Timminy and I are glad to see each other. That's all."

"Abby!" said Becca.

"Spit it out," said Carver.

"If I have to, I'll have a duel with you, crutch to cane, Abby Winslow, to get it out of you," said Devon.

Abby didn't make them wait any longer. She shouted so loud, I wondered if even Maxi could have heard her.

"I'M GETTING A GUIDE DOG!"

What a pig pile!

Everyone hugged Abby at the same time. I was in the middle, along with Abby. We were all laughing and screaming and cheering.

A teacher tried to yell over us. "Break it up! Break it up!" She thought it was a fight. But when we separated and stepped back from Abby, I saw Dad put his hand on the teacher's shoulder and say, "It's okay. I've got this."

Then he said, "Resume your celebration, everyone. Congratulations, Abby! And if anyone needs a late pass to homeroom, I'll have a stack ready in my office." He turned and left. That's *my* dad, I thought. One of Abby's parents must have told him the news.

Just then Rory walked up. He towered above everyone and demanded, "What's going on?"

Everyone instinctively took a step back, except Abby. She took a step toward Rory, lifted her head proudly, and said, "I'm getting a guide dog, A GUIDE DOG, Rory!"

Rory did what I could only attempt minutes before. He picked Abby up like she was a teddy bear and swung her around and around and around.

"Whoa!" Abby said when he put her down, all wobbly.

"Sorry," said Rory. "I'm just happy for you, Ab-B-B-B."

"Thanks," said Abby.

I asked a question I hadn't dared to ask before. "What's Ab-B-B-B mean?"

Rory said, "It's my nickname for her—the *b*'s are for blind, black, and . . . beautiful!"

Abby smiled the biggest smile. Maybe it was because Rory called her "beautiful." Maybe it was because she was finally getting her dream—a guide dog.

I led Abby to her homeroom and said, "See you later, Ab-B-B-B-B!"

"Why the extra *b*?"

"For brave."

Her smile grew even bigger.

That's how I knew Abby's answer from MIRA was a yes! Because she was brave enough to come to school *without* her dark glasses.

Look out, world, here comes Abby Winslow!

SECRET #38
What a feeling—when the world finally says yes to you!

CHAPTER 39

HOW COULD A *yes!* turn into an *oh no!* so fast?

Maybe it's one of those laws like "What goes up must come down." And when your world comes crashing down on top of you, you're not sure you'll ever be strong enough to lift it.

It started like a regular Saturday. I ran errands with Dad to the pet shop to get Maxi more treats and dog food. Then we went to the hardware store to pick up a couple of shovels.

The first snow of the year was forecast for that afternoon. It was early December and everyone was complaining it was so late this year—the hunters didn't have a trace of snow for tracking deer during hunting season in November. Last year the first snow had been in October.

After the hardware store, we went to the grocery store to stock up on "snow food." We were only supposed to get three to six inches, but since it was the first snow, the grocery store was packed. I guess people in this part of Maine liked to be prepared (or maybe they knew something about snowstorms we city folks didn't).

Dad and I got stuff to make a big pan of lasagna and homemade biscuits—the Winslows were coming to supper. We also stopped at Fudge Fantasy and got two pounds of fudge for dessert. (Mom said it had better last for a week or we'd have bellyaches—she didn't realize Abby and I knew how to hold our fudge!)

I was trying to hurry Dad through all the errands. I'd promised Abby I'd make it back so Maxi and I could take her for a walk in the woods before it snowed. We probably wouldn't get to go in the woods again until spring, after the snow melted. And by then, Abby would hopefully have her own guide dog to take her. Walking in the woods with our two dogs would be fun, but Abby warned me not to hold my breath, "Wintah in this paht of Maine can last fah-evah—ayuh!" (Abby could *really* pour on the Maine accent when she wanted.)

As Dad drove back home, it was already spitting snow, and the radio gave an update:

The storm has intensified and tracked further west than originally predicted. We are now under a Winter Storm Warning and eight to twelve inches of snow are expected by this evening, falling at a rate of one to two inches per hour at the storm's peak. Travel will quickly become dangerous. Stay tuned for further updates and cancellations.

Dad said, "Kind of exciting—our first snowfall in Skenago."

I nodded. I was anxious to see Maxi's reaction to snow. I hoped I wouldn't lose my big white dog in a big white snowdrift.

Dad continued, "Good thing the Winslows live close enough to still come over for supper even with the snow coming in."

As we pulled into the garage, I told Dad I'd be back to help him unload the car in a few minutes. I raced inside and upstairs to call Abby on FaceTime. She didn't pick up so I sent her an email:

A—

Got home later and snow started earlier so no woods walk today. Sorry! See you for supper.
FYI, got fudge!

—T

I ran back downstairs to help Dad, but he already had the car unpacked and was putting groceries away along with Mom. They shooed me outside to check out the snow with Maxi.

As soon as we stepped out the door, Maxi looked up as if to say, "What the heck? The sky is falling?" She opened her mouth and snowflakes fell on her tongue. She barked her approval and then opened her mouth again. Snow was already sticking to the frozen grass. She stuck her snout in the snow and then shook it off. She kept leaping from place to place and putting her snout in the snow over and over again. Then she lifted her snout straight up in the air and sent snow flying, like she was tossing white confetti.

My parents came out to watch and laugh at Maxi too. Mom said, "She reminds me of you, Timminy, when you were a toddler and played out in the snow the first time. Such wonder!"

Next, Maxi lay down and rolled on her back, squirming every which way. Her Pyr fur coat that made her so hot in the summer now kept her warm as she rolled around in the snow. She loved it. I wasn't sure we'd ever get her back inside.

Brrrrng-brrrrng! Dad's cell phone.

"It's for you, Timminy. Mrs. Winslow." Dad passed me his phone.

Mrs. Winslow's voice sounded strained. "Timminy, is Abby with you?"

"No, I haven't seen her yet today."

"Did she tell you her plans? Bruce and I ran errands and when we got home, we assumed Abby was in her room. But we hollered for her to come to lunch, and she didn't answer. We checked. She's not there. We checked the whole house. She's not anywhere. We were hoping she was with you."

"She's not."

"Did she tell you what she was doing today?"

I swallowed hard and now my voice sounded strained. "Um, we'd talked about going for a walk in the woods."

"*Not* in the snow?"

"No, we thought we could get a walk in before the snow arrived, but it started earlier and I got home later from running errands with my dad."

My parents stared at me, looking worried as they pieced things together from my side of the conversation.

I swallowed hard and said, "But, Mrs. Winslow, sometimes Abby goes for walks by herself in the woods."

There was silence on the other end. I didn't know if Mrs. Winslow had dropped the phone or fainted or what.

I looked at Dad, nodded, and said, "We'll be right over."

Mom made Dad and me come inside to bundle up before we headed over to the Winslows'. She said she'd head over later if we didn't find Abby right off, but for now she was going to start cooking so we'd all have something hot to eat when we got back.

I wanted to take Maxi with us. Mom insisted, "No!"

But I was willing to fight the Boss on this one. "She's coming with us, Mom. Maxi has a super sense of smell, and she's the only search dog we've got."

Mom still wasn't convinced. "But she's deaf."

"She has her pager collar, and she's not blind. She can look for Abby. And she's found her way out of the woods before when *I* couldn't."

Now both my parents looked at me.

Dad started, "You were lost in the woods, Timminy? And you never told—"

Mom interrupted him. I figured she'd finish what he'd started, but instead she said, "Kenneth, obviously Timminy got himself found. There's no time for this. Abby's missing. You three need to go find her."

Three? She said *three*, so Maxi could come too.

I grabbed my mittens and hat, put on my boots, and thought about grabbing treats to coax Maxi along during the search, but I didn't bother.

Maxi didn't need a reward to look for Abby.

It was Abby!

SECRET #39
Maybe it *was* possible for the sky to fall.

CHAPTER 40

ABBY'S MOM WAS waiting for us and said, "Bruce is out back—"

I interrupted. "Let's call her cell phone! Abby always has it with her."

Mrs. Winslow whispered, "I did. I called her before I called you. No answer, it went to her voice mail. I left her a message. She hasn't called back."

I shivered, and not because of the cold and snow. Abby *always* had her phone. What'd happened?

Dad jumped in. "What about her cane? Is that missing?"

"Yes," said Mrs. Winslow.

"Good," said Dad.

Mrs. Winslow tried to nod. I understood. The cane was maybe a little bit of good news, but not really. Mrs. Winslow and I both knew Abby too well. Something had happened, and she might need more than her cane to get her out of trouble.

"I've called the sheriff's department. They're on their way and they've notified local game wardens. I'll wait here for them."

"We'll go help Bruce," Dad said. He put his hand on Mrs. Winslow's shoulder to make her feel better, parent to parent. I gave Dad credit for trying, but even I know parents can't feel better when their kids are in trouble.

I tugged Maxi toward the backyard, then spun around. "Have you called Rory yet? You should. He hunts and really knows these woods."

Mrs. Winslow and Dad looked at each other and said, "Good idea."

As we walked around their house, I looked up at the snow coming down harder, like someone was shaking a snow globe and we were inside it. I looked behind us and saw our footprints. Maybe that would help. If only we could find Abby's footprints before the snow covered them up.

When we got out back, Mr. Winslow was yelling and pausing, yelling and pausing—pausing to hear Abby's response, which didn't come.

He grabbed my arm. "Do you know which way she's gone into the woods before? I've been waiting for you to tell me where before I head in."

Dad put his hand over Mr. Winslow's to release his grip from me and said, "Easy, Bruce. Do you think we should be going in before the sheriff's department and game wardens get here? Will it be harder for them to find her if our footprints are mixed up in there too?"

Mr. Winslow moved his pointing finger to Dad's chest and tapped it in rhythm to his words. "What . . . if . . . it . . . were . . . YOUR . . . kid?"

Dad dropped his eyes. "You're right. Let's go. Which way, Timminy?"

Everything looked different in the snow. It was sticking to trees and bushes, making odd, ghostly shapes. I wasn't sure where to go. And anyway, I was the one who had gotten lost before—no one should trust me. I was going to say that when I felt a pull, a strong pull.

I looked down and saw Maxi tugging.

"Maxi knows," I said. "Let's follow her." And we did.

We headed into the woods. The snow wasn't as deep in there yet. Some of the pine trees acted like giant umbrellas protecting the ground from snow (but it wasn't long before those umbrellas dumped snow on us as the branches became too heavy). We stopped every ten feet and hollered, all three of us, "Abby! Abby! Abby!" Then we held our breath and waited. Nothing. By then Maxi was straining against her leash again. She knew we had farther to go.

We kept walking ten feet, stopping to holler, no answer.

Walking ten feet, stopping to holler, no answer.

Over and over, until . . .

Maxi barked and nudged something under the snow with her snout.

We looked down and I could feel it. Two grown men and one short boy wanted to do the same thing—cry.

Maxi had found Abby's phone.

Mr. Winslow picked it up and cradled it in his gloved hands as if he were holding a piece of his daughter, but it wasn't a piece of her.

My dad cleared his throat. "At least now we know she's out here, Bruce." Dad meant well, but I couldn't imagine his words were any comfort to Mr. Winslow. They didn't comfort me.

Finding Abby's phone was a gut punch. Part of me had hoped she was asleep under her covers or reading a braille book in her closet and her parents had somehow missed her when they'd looked.

The idea of her being out in these woods alone in a snowstorm was a nightmare, a nightmare that was now real.

We didn't say anything more, not to one another. There was nothing to say. We shouted, "Abby! Abby! Abby!" out into the storm as we kept following Maxi's lead. Maxi was our hope. She wanted to find Abby as much as we did, and she seemed to be on her trail.

All of a sudden, sounds blasted at us from opposite directions.

"Anyone there? This is the Warden Service."
Vroom-vroom-vroom!

The first sound squawked from a bullhorn. The Warden Service, the expert searchers, had arrived to search for Abby. A relief.

The second sound—Rory's ATV. Mrs. Winslow must have reached him. Somehow that was a bigger relief to me—he knew these woods and he'd do anything for Abby.

There was a third sound too, but I was the only one who heard it. A little whine, more like a whimper. I looked down. It was Maxi. She looked up at me with begging eyes. I knew what she was telling me. She wanted to go find Abby, and we were holding her back.

The snow was falling harder and visibility was getting poorer, but I felt like I could see things more clearly than I had since we'd started searching.

I cleared my throat, hoping they'd listen to me even though I was little. "Dad, why don't you follow our footsteps back to where we found Abby's phone and stay there so the wardens will know that's the last known location for her." Dad nodded.

I continued, "Mr. Winslow, head toward the sound of the warden's bullhorn. Lead them back to Dad and tell them Maxi is on to Abby's scent, but we haven't found her yet." Mr. Winslow nodded.

I gulped. Were they really going to listen to me?

Finally, I said, "I'm heading toward the *vroom*. It's Rory on his ATV. He knows these woods. Maybe he's seen something or has ideas where to look. I'll update him on what we've found . . . haven't found."

Dad and Mr. Winslow looked at each other as if to ask, *Got a better plan?*

Mr. Winslow spoke first, "Here, Timminy. We have our cell phones, but you don't have one. Take Abby's." He clicked it to see if it still worked after sitting in the snow. How long had it been on the ground? It did seem to work. So maybe it hadn't been too long.

Dad said, "Good idea, Bruce. Are you sure you can find Rory, Timminy? I don't need you missing too."

"Yes, Dad. He'll be on the wide trail up ahead. I'll just follow the sound of his engine. Plus I have Maxi. If I can't find Rory, I'll have Maxi lead me back to Abby's house." He couldn't see my fingers crossed inside my mittens.

Dad nodded, then reached out to give me a hug. We each headed off in our separate directions. When we were far enough away, I leaned down and lifted Maxi's snout to look her right in the eyes. *Are you sure, girl?* She whined. I knew her answer, but I wanted to hear it again. *Okay, I trust you. Tell Abby I sent you.* I put Abby's phone in front of her snout for a final sniff, to remind her of the treasure she was searching for. But she didn't need a reminder. She knew. She whined once more, then leaned in, and gave me one of her hugs as I kissed the top of her head.

She ran off. Just like that she was gone, her whiteness blending into the falling snow.

I tried following in the direction she'd gone. But I couldn't keep up, and soon her paw prints were covered by snow (must be the one–two inches per hour they'd predicted). I still stopped and hollered every ten steps, "Abby! Abby! Maxi!" Maxi couldn't hear me, but I needed to say her name 'cause I was looking for her too. I waited and listened. Nothing.

It was easier walking on the wide trail. I saw tire tracks in the snow that I figured must be from Rory's ATV. Tire tracks were bigger, deeper, easier to follow than a dog's paw prints. I had no idea if Abby had wandered onto the wide trail. Still, I stayed on it since I didn't know which way to go and I'd only get myself lost.

LOST!

That word pounced on me. I tried to shake it off, but it had already dug in its claws. *What if you lost both of them? Abby and Maxi? It'll be your fault, you know.*

ALL.

YOUR.

FAULT.

You weren't there for Abby when you promised her one more walk. And you let Maxi go into a storm, into danger—ALONE.

LOST!
BOTH LOST!
FOREVER LOST!

I balled up my fists inside my mittens and swung and swung at those words flying around my head.

"SHUT UP!" I screamed. "I don't care what you say. Leave me alone. I'm not playing your games anymore. I'm *not* feeling sorry for myself—I have stuff to do.

GOTTA.

FIND.

MY.

GIRLS!"

I stomped through the snow and headed in the direction I thought Maxi had gone. I couldn't be sure. But I was sure I was doing my best and that's all I could do.

SECRET #40
There's no guarantee your best is good enough.

CHAPTER 41

THE SNOW SEEMED lighter, or maybe somehow I was.

I kept walking and yelling, stopping and listening. I knew if Maxi had found Abby and she was within range that she'd bark to let me know where she was.

As I strained to listen, a familiar sound grew and grew. *Vroom-vroom-vroom!*

It sounded like the other beast, Rory. I'd lost his engine sound for a while, but now he was getting closer. And closer!

But I didn't jump out of his way this time. I waved both arms like crazy, so he'd see me, so he'd stop, before he ran over me.

He jammed on his brakes. I slammed my eyes shut. Ready for the impact . . .

A BLAST OF SNOW!

I opened my eyes, and for the first time was eyeball to eyeball with Rory Pelletier, as he sat and I stood. I glanced down. Three inches to spare before he'd have hit me. I figured he'd yell at me and he did, but not what I expected.

"Jump on, Minny! Abby! Last chance!"

Rory raced on the wide trail for a quarter mile or so, then made a sharp left turn onto a narrow trail. Snowy, droopy branches smacked us, or rather smacked Rory. He was so big—he took all the hits, but then I got all the snow in my face.

Rory killed the engine and jumped off. He pulled off his gloves and shoved them into his pocket, then reached up and grabbed a box strapped to a tree. He pushed a button and a little square fell into his palm. I recognized an SD card that cameras use. He closed his hand over the SD card to keep it dry as he reached inside his jacket with his other hand. He pulled out what looked like a handheld video game with a screen and a camouflage pattern around the edge. He slipped the SD card inside and pushed a switch. Rory was so tall I couldn't look over his shoulder to see what he was seeing so I watched his face instead.

That's when I knew *last chance* meant "hopeful."

Rory didn't waste words. "Abby—fifty minutes ago. Maxi—fifteen minutes ago. Both—thatta way." He pointed deeper into the woods, down a narrow path heading away from the wide trail. Then he started *walking* thatta way.

I had done a good job not asking questions that would slow us down. But I couldn't muzzle this question, "Why the heck don't we take your ATV?"

"Too fast. We'd miss clues. Too loud. We wouldn't hear them."

So I trudged behind Rory, trying to stay up with him.

"Look left. I've got right," he said.

I stared left so hard my eyeballs ached, but all I saw was snow. Snow covered everything.

But then Rory shouted, "There!" I looked right, and the snow had some indents.

"ABBY!" Rory shouted.

We froze—our bodies, our breaths.

No answer.

Rory stepped farther to the right and again, "ABBY!"

No answer.

"Dang!" Rory said. "Dogs have better hearing than people, but Maxi's deaf. She's no help."

"Don't be so sure," I said.

Rory looked confused as I pulled the controller to Maxi's collar out of my pocket and triggered it. Again and again.

Then we heard it! We both heard it! A bark! Maxi's bark!

We raced in the direction of the barking. My legs were shorter, but that didn't stop me from passing Rory. Maxi's bark was like a turbo-boost to me.

There!

Down a deep gully.

Maxi was still barking as she covered Abby's body with her body.

Oh no! Body! Please, please, Abby has to be more than a body.

Rory and I both screamed, "ABBY!"

First, a laugh bubbled up, and then, "What took you two so long?"

Rory and I threw our arms around each other and did a happy dance. (Don't tell anyone, but we did!)

Then we half walked, half stumbled down the side of the gully.

Only when we reached them did Maxi get off Abby.

"Phew!" she said. "Talk about a guard dog—she barely left me space to breathe, lying on me to keep me warm."

"Are you okay?" I asked.

"It's my ankle, twisted it when I fell." But as Rory brushed aside some snow to look at it . . .

Bee-bop-bing! Bee-bop-bing! My pocket started to vibrate.

"My phone!" yelled Abby. "You found it!"

"Maxi did."

Her phone screen showed who was calling. "It's your dad, Abby," I said.

"Tell him I'm okay."

"*You* tell him." I passed her the phone.

When she clicked to answer the call, we could hear her father yelling, "TIMMINY, I'M WITH THE GAME WARDENS. WE FOUND RORY'S ABANDONED ATV. WHERE THE HECK ARE YOU?"

Abby's voice was quieter than I'd ever heard it before. "He's with me, Daddy. He's with me."

I don't know if the next sound I heard through the phone was a sob or a scream or a sigh—probably all three at the same time.

I leaned down and buried my face in Maxi's fur. I knew exactly how Abby's dad felt.

SECRET #41
Lost and found—there's nothing like the *found* feeling.

CHAPTER 42

IT WAS LIKE we were in the middle of a live-action survival movie—watching it and acting in it, all at the same time.

First things first—Abby. The game wardens showed up with Mr. Winslow. They were pretty sure her ankle wasn't broken, but they still carried her out of the gully on a stretcher, wrapped her in blankets, and pulled her out on a sled behind one of their snowmobiles. Mr. Winslow was on the warden's second snowmobile. He wouldn't let Abby out of his sight.

That left Rory, Maxi, and me. The wardens said they'd be back for us, but Rory said, "Don't bother. We're all set."

But as the wardens sped off, we realized we weren't quite all set. Maxi was limping again. Maybe she'd twisted her ankle too going down the gully. We'd been so focused on Abby, we hadn't noticed.

"She's riding with me, Minny."

"So that leaves me lost in the woods?"

"Nah."

Rory sent a text on his phone, then said, "I'll wait till your ride gets here."

Soon a snowmobile zoomed up, and for a second I thought Rory had a twin. But then the bulky driver lifted his helmet—Kevin Cole, my booster-seat buddy.

"NOT him!" we shouted at the same time.

"Shut up, both of you!" Rory put his pointing finger in my face. "I'm giving Maxi a ride. She's hurt. You're not. So you're going with Kevin or walking."

I nodded.

Then he raised that finger a couple of feet and put it in Kevin's face. But before Rory could say anything, Kevin shoved Rory's finger aside. "Your text said *you* needed a ride. Not this pipsqueak. I hate pipsqueaks."

Rory turned his pointing finger into a fist and held it an inch from Kevin's nose. "I said 'Shut up!' And grow up! So Minny here's a pipsqueak—get used to it. You can be ONE BIG JERK—I'm used to it."

I closed my eyes expecting fists to fly. Would they kill each other?

But then I heard a snort and opened my eyes to see Rory had Kevin in a headlock and was giving him a noogie. And Kevin was snorting too.

Woof! Woof! Maxi barked at them and jumped off Rory's ATV. Her limp looked worse.

I put both my fists up and said, "Let's go or you'd better get used to these."

Rory nearly fell over laughing. He pushed my fists down, threw me over his shoulder, and put me on the back of Kevin's snowmobile. Then he picked up Maxi and got on his ATV, holding her gently yet firmly as he zoomed away.

Kevin grumbled. For a second, I thought about being a wise-mouth and saying something about him *really* being a Big Jerk. But instead I took a deep breath and waited. Kevin's grumble turned into a sigh, then he pushed down his helmet, and we zoomed off after Rory.

When we pulled into the Winslows' backyard, everything was chaos.

Dad was by the edge of the woods waiting. He grabbed me for a hug. "You're okay," he said, relieved. I knew I was okay so I pulled away.

"How's Abby? Maxi?" I asked.

"Abby's getting checked at the health clinic. Rory brought Maxi to our house. Mom's warming her up, checking her over."

I looked at Dad, closer, trying to figure out his expression. Worry! I knew that feeling. So I leaned into him for a real hug this time.

The rest of the world started to come into focus.

People were yelling to me.

"Timminy, you okay?"

"Good news on Abby."

"Your dog's a hero."

"You too, and Rory."

The Winslows' backyard was filled with ATVs and snowmobiles, and kids I knew, ones I didn't know, and grown-ups too. I think some of them belonged with the kids. And there were game wardens and sheriff's deputies too.

A reporter from the local paper was interviewing everyone about what had happened. Carver and Kassy, the student council prez, seemed to be answering most of the questions. When they brought the reporter toward me, I waved them off. "You've got this." They both smiled, and Kassy didn't even pat me on the head.

Dad borrowed a bullhorn from one of the game wardens. "Everyone, on behalf of the Winslows, I'd like to thank all of you for coming out in big numbers in a big storm to help find Abby."

Everyone cheered.

"And a special thanks to the sheriff's department and game wardens."

Bigger cheers.

"And our dog, Maxi, and my son, Timminy, and especially Rory."

The biggest cheers.

Dad continued. "The storm is letting up. So if anyone

is hungry, my wife has cooked up some vittles at our house next door and you're all welcome."

Rory nudged me with his elbow. (How long had he been there?) "Vittles? What the heck are vittles?"

"Food, Rory, *food*. And if you really want to know more, my dad can tell you what century the word *vittles* originated and what Old English or Latin word it derived from."

"Not interested." Rory rolled his eyes. "Just wanna know if your mom is a better cook than Abby's."

"I know it doesn't look like I eat much," I told him, "but I do. I stuff my face every day. My mom's a good cook. So's my dad."

And with that, Rory slapped Kevin on the back. "Race you to Mr. AP's house."

Kevin looked at me, not sure if he was invited, not sure if he wanted to be.

I shrugged and said, "My dad said everyone. Guess that includes Big Jerks."

Rory snorted. Kevin didn't. But they both jumped on their machines, along with a bunch of other kids and grown-ups, and raced over to our house for vittles.

I wondered two things . . .

If Mom knew how many people Dad was inviting for vittles.

And if there'd be a tiny bite of fudge left for Abby

and me to share by the time this search party had searched out all the food at our house.

SECRET #42
You may not have to look very far to find more than what you were searching for.

CHAPTER 43

OUR HOUSE HAD never had so many people in it. There was a giant heap of boots and shoes by the front door—everyone trying not to track in a mess. When I hung up my coat in the laundry room, I found an over-flowing pile of coats, mittens, and gloves on top of our washer and dryer. I wasn't sure how everyone would sort out this jumble when they left. Maybe it didn't mat-ter as long as everyone ended up with some winter gear.

I squeezed past all the bodies and slaps on the back and the buzz of words:

"Way to go."

"How was Abby when you found her?"

"Nice of your folks."

"Where's your hero dog?"

My hero dog was *next*. But first—Mom.

I knew she'd be in the middle of the kitchen chaos. I excused myself as I scrunched between bodies until I got to her. Her back was to me when I tapped her on the shoulder and said, "Mom."

"Timminy," she squealed. She threw her arms around me and pulled me in tight. "Oh, Timminy." Then she pulled back to look me over, to be sure I still had all my body parts. I knew what was next so I beat her to it and hugged her back even harder than she'd hugged me. I heard some *aww*s but I didn't mind. Mom needed that hug.

"Eat, Timminy, eat. You must be starved. Let me fix you a plate."

"In a bit, Mom. Where's Maxi? I want to check on her first."

"In your room where Rory carried her to keep her out of all this commotion."

"How's she doing? Should we take her to the vet's?"

"Let's watch her and let her get some rest. She's only limping a little. We can take her in on Monday if we need to."

"Okay," I said. "I will take that plate after all."

Mom smiled and passed me one ready on the counter—she had been filling plate after plate to hand to everyone—but she heaped even more on the one she gave me. I saw the food that she made, lasagna and biscuits, but there was lots more stuff too. For the first time, I realized not only had many helped with the search, but also many others had brought food.

It was tricky balancing a plate and making my way through the crowd and up the stairs. Kevin was standing bodyguard, er . . . puppyguard outside my bedroom door. He stepped aside and opened the door since I was holding the heaping plate with both hands.

He snorted and grabbed two biscuits off the top.

When Kevin shut the door after me, I heard a cooing sound.

"Such a good puppy. Such a good Little Beast."

HACK-HACK! I cleared my throat. Rory was lying on my bed with Maxi, who was sound asleep.

Rory jumped up. "Oh, it's you."

"And *for* you," I said, passing him the plate. "How's she doing?"

"Better, I think. Just needs some rest. She worked harder than the rest of us."

Rory took the plate I offered. "I already had one plate, but fresh air makes me hungry."

He started chowing down. "Wait!" I said. I reached up and grabbed the cheese chunks. "Those are for Maxi."

Rory opened the door and said, "Your mom *is* a good cook. I'm gonna go get dessert"—he stared at Kevin and finished—"before some pig eats it all." The door slammed, and I heard giant stomps racing down the stairs and toward the kitchen.

I lay down next to Maxi and held a cheese chunk up to her nose. She stirred, opened her eyes, gulped the cheese, then licked my hand. I was certain it wasn't because of the leftover cheese smell on my fingers, but to show me I was still her favorite, no matter how much Rory cooed to her. I fed her more cheese, and after the last bite, she cut a cheese fart—her way of saying thanks.

"You're welcome, girl."

Later that night, my dad and I went to check on Abby. She was lying on the couch with her leg propped up on a pillow and ice bags hugging her ankle. She had scratches on her face and hands. I hadn't noticed those before.

"How you feeling?" I asked her.

"Sore and tired, but I'll live."

"Thanks for the warning," I said.

Abby reached out and smacked me with the throw pillow she'd had on her lap. "Take that," she said.

"That's all you've got to give?"

She laughed. "It really is." She pointed at her ankle. "I can't kick you. And I lost my cane in the woods so I can't even trip you."

"Uh-oh! I forgot about your cane. Rory and I can go look for it tomorrow."

"NO!" said my dad.

"NO!" echoed Abby's parents. "We'll get her a new one."

I figured it was best to change the subject.

"Here," I said. "I saved you some fudge." She opened her hand, took the fudge, and smelled it. "*Mmmmm*, one of my favorites, finger-lickin' Butterfinger. Want half?" She broke it and held a piece out to me.

"*Snot* me," I said.

She smacked me again with the pillow, then popped both chunks into her mouth. "Yum!"

I was too tired to keep up our teasing, so I propped the pillow Abby had hit me with under my head and lay on the floor with my eyes closed as I listened to Abby and our dads do a play-by-play . . .

Abby had heard the snow was coming in earlier. She thought she could still get in a short walk before it started even though I wasn't back to join her. When it started snowing, she turned back. She also decided to call her parents since she didn't want them to worry. But when she reached for her phone, it wasn't there. She figured it must have fallen out of her pocket earlier when her hands had gotten cold and she'd pulled out her mittens. That's when she panicked. The phone was expensive and with a new guide dog on the way, she didn't want her parents to have to buy her a new phone—or worse, maybe they wouldn't buy her one.

So she got down on the ground, trying to retrace where she'd walked and find her phone. But crawling, instead of walking while trying to hang on to her cane, everything seemed all mixed up. She decided she should probably stay in one place until someone found her—she figured I'd put things together and realize where she was and come looking. But it was snowing harder and she got so cold standing still, she started walking again in what she *hoped* was the right direction.

When she heard a snorting sound, she got scared. She knew it was an animal, a big animal, probably a moose. She heard a *CRASH* and thought the animal was running after her. So she ran in the opposite direction, tripped on a tree root, and tumbled into the gully. When she tried to stand, she realized she'd hurt her ankle. So she sat back and waited. Abby wasn't sure how long she was there before she heard Maxi bark at the top of the gully and then scamper down to her. Abby said, "Timminy, you know the rest of the story."

But before I could say anything, Dad said, "But you don't know what everyone else was doing to find you, Abby." So he told us how the game wardens had a map of the area and had set up a grid search. They even had search dogs coming from Bangor.

Abby said, "I only needed one search dog—Maxi. Wait! Why didn't you bring her over with you, Timminy?"

"She's even more tired than we are, Abby. I'll bring her over tomorrow."

"And maybe she can tell us her side of the story." Abby laughed.

"To be continued," said Mrs. Winslow with a big yawn.

We all yawned in agreement.

SECRET #43
Life is one big story, with some chapters more exciting—and more scary—than others.

CHAPTER 44

ON SUNDAY, RORY came over to check on Maxi.

"How's my Little Beast doing?" he cooed at her.

"Better. Limping less, but we're going to take her to the vet's tomorrow to get her checked," I said.

"Good." He leaned down and rubbed his thumb along her snout.

"Um, Rory, you do know Maxi is *my* dog—not yours?"

"Yeah," he said with a sigh. "My mom was allergic to dogs so we never had one. And when she left, Dad said his workdays were too long for a dog to be home alone."

"Try getting on your knees and begging your dad," I suggested. "It always works for me."

"Like this?" Rory dropped to his knees and snorted. "I'm still taller than you."

I couldn't help but laugh at the big oaf.

"Well, I better go check on Abby." Rory stood up,

stepped toward the door, then stopped. "Hey, it's lunchtime. Does your mom have any of that lasagna left from yesterday?"

I laughed. "Nope, *some* people had three or four helpings."

"So what's she cooking today?"

"It's Sunday—it's my dad's day to cook."

Rory sighed. "Guess I'll see what cans Abby's mom is opening up."

"I'll check to see if it's okay if you stay for lunch."

"But your dad is cooking."

"Yeah, he's a good cook."

I don't think Rory believed me, but then he wolfed down three bowls of Dad's beef stew.

While he was scraping the bottom of his third bowl, I saw my mom mouth to my dad, *Bye-bye, leftovers.*

Maybe she was getting revenge on Rory when she said, "All right, Timminy, it's time for your parents' Sunday newspaper interlude. You and Rory can clean up and do the dishes."

Rory jumped up and said, "We got this, Mrs. Harris," as he started clearing the table.

Before Mom and Dad disappeared into the den, I said, "Rory's gonna go check on Abby afterward. Can I go with him?"

Dad, forever the English major, said, "*May* you?"

Mom rolled her eyes. "Yes, you can and *may* after

you do the dishes and after you take Maxi out to do her business."

I looked at Rory. He nodded. Then I looked back at Mom and said, "We got this."

She playfully smacked me and then Rory with the rolled-up Sunday newspaper before disappearing into the den with Dad.

"I'll wash. You wipe," said Rory.

I laughed. "You big oaf, we just have to put stuff in the dishwasher and start it."

"Who you calling a big oaf?" Rory leaned down in my face.

"I am! The Shrimp is calling you a Big Oaf."

Rory laughed. "Actually, I prefer Beast of the East, or Shrek."

"That all you got for names? You've lived a deprived life. I have a bunch . . . Tiny Tim, Peewee, Peanut, Wee-wee . . . for starters."

"RHAAAAAH!" Rory started to stomp around the kitchen. "I am the Jolly Mean Giant."

"Out of my kitchen, Jolly Mean Giant and Peewee Harris!" said my mom as she appeared in the doorway.

"Yes, ma'am"—Rory looked embarrassed—but as we headed out, he said, "Tiny Tim started it." And we all couldn't stop laughing.

Outside, Maxi was still intrigued with the snow and

kept tossing it with her snout, which amused Rory. He agreed her limp seemed better.

"Rory, lucky for Abby you have your trail camera. Do you use it when you hunt?"

"Hunt?" Rory asked.

"Yeah, when you hunt."

"I don't hunt."

I didn't want to ruin Rory's and my newfound we've-both-been-called-names camaraderie, but I couldn't help myself. "You said you shot animals."

"What the heck are you talking about, Wee-wee?"

I knew what I knew. "I was in your driveway once and I heard you say you had to check what you'd shot."

Rory leaned down and moved his face within inches of mine, "You been spying on me?"

"No, I was trying to avoid you, Shrek. I was looking for Abby's house when we first moved here, and I didn't know where she lived. I went up your driveway by mistake—that's when I heard you talk about what you'd shot."

Rory looked puzzled for a second, then snorted.

"Let me in on the joke," I said.

"Shot animals with my trail cams to video them, to see them, not shot—*bang-bang* dead."

"But I thought lots of kids around here hunt."

"They do. Not me."

"You seem the type."

"I might have been," said Rory. "But my dad almost lost his eye in a BB gun accident when he was a kid so he's always had a no-hunting rule for him and me and my brother."

I shook my head. It's amazing how much you don't know about somebody you don't know. I was past worrying about being too nosy so I asked Rory a bunch of questions. And found out Rory hadn't seen his mom since she moved to Arizona three years ago, and he was saving money to buy more trail camcorders to study all the wildlife out in the woods. He already had three cams. Yesterday he had checked the two set up closest to the ponds first since water would have been the worst place for Abby to be lost. He was also saving money for a fancy camera with a zoom lens. He'd built tree stands to take photos of animals—he wanted to be a wildlife photographer.

All I could say was something my mom sometimes says: "Who'd have thunk it?"

Rory just snorted.

SECRET #44

Life is not only full of little *Minny* surprises, but big *Oaf* surprises too.

CHAPTER 45

THE NEXT DAY, Mom took Maxi to the vet's. I tried to convince her I should stay home and go with them, but she said, "I got this."

Dad and I went to school. I knew Abby wouldn't be there. When Rory and I had checked on her the day before, she was doing better, but still needed to stay off her ankle a few more days. Crutches and blindness were *not* a good mix.

Too bad Abby missed school because all everyone was talking about was Abby getting lost (or maybe she wouldn't have wanted to be the center of attention). Since she wasn't there, Rory and I got a lot of the attention and questions. Dad even gave an update over the intercom during morning announcements.

At lunch, Carver proudly showed off a copy of the newspaper with the article about the rescue and a couple of photos. He'd circled the photo where the reporter was interviewing him plus the two places in the article that quoted him. He said, "I brought extra copies for you and Abby, Timminy. Can you bring her a copy?"

"Sure," I said, trying to keep a straight face as I saw the copies for Abby and me also had the references to Carver circled and highlighted—so we wouldn't miss *him*.

Lunch was finishing when Dad showed up. "Come with me, Timminy." He looked serious, too serious. I followed him and asked, "What's wrong?"

"Just grab your coat. We'll talk in the car."

"We're leaving? *You're* leaving? You've never missed a minute of school."

"Well, the place will have to survive without me for the afternoon. Come on."

"Should I bring my books?"

Dad shook his head. "Just your coat."

Man, he was freaking me out. Freaking me out by what he *didn't* say.

When I jumped into the car, I said, "Tell me. Is it Mom?"

"No."

"Maxi?"

He nodded as a single tear trickled down his cheek. He wiped it fast, not wanting me to see it, but I did and it was too late to take back that tear. Too late to make everything okay again.

Dad shot straight with me then. "Your mother got back from the vet's. Maxi's limping—it's not from an injury. It's bone cancer. We're going to take her to Portland now for a second opinion."

I turned my head to the window. I wasn't sure how Dad had limited himself to *one* tear, 'cause my eyes gushed. "Not Maxi. It's not fair." I felt Dad's hand on my shoulder, but he didn't say anything.

There wasn't anything he could say.

The rest of the day was a blur or maybe blurry as my eyes wouldn't dry up.

We went to Portland to see a specialist vet who confirmed Maxi had osteosarcoma. That fancy word didn't change anything. It was still bone cancer.

Pieces of conversation tried to push through my fog . . .

"Yes, it's unusual for a dog so young to have bone cancer, but not unheard of in giant breeds."

"It's in her left hind leg and has moved to her lungs, too, so there's no real treatment."

"The cancer will destroy her bones from the inside out until she can't walk anymore."

"Yes, it hurts. And the pain will get worse over time."

"You'll know when it's time. She has weeks. If you're lucky, maybe a few months."

Maxi was sleeping on the ride back from Portland after the medicine they'd given her to keep her still for the X-rays and biopsy. I held on to her the whole way, as tight as I could without hurting her. And it's a good thing she had lots of thick fur, to absorb lots of tears.

When we got home, I had an email from Abby. Devon had called and told her I'd left school early, and she wanted to know what was going on.

I told my parents, "Sit with Maxi while I go tell Abby."

Dad said, "I can go tell the Winslows."

"No, I need to."

Mom said, "Want one of us to go with you?"

"No, please sit with Maxi until I get back."

And that's what they did.

While I did what I did.

And what Abby did was cry. And cry some more.

"I need to get back to Maxi. But I wanted you to know, Abby."

"This stinks," said Abby, "but I'm glad you're the one who told me."

SECRET #45
The bad stuff, like the good stuff, needs to be shared.

CHAPTER 46

I LET THE NEWS about Maxi settle in for a few days before I told anyone else. Although everyone knew something was wrong.

"You sick?"

"Worried about Abby? She'll be back at school any day."

"Did someone shut you in a locker again?"

I just shrugged each time. I ate alone with a book at lunch—staring at the page, not reading. Carver came and sat with me, but he didn't say anything (maybe he was more aware than I gave him credit for). He just read a book. Rory nodded at me whenever he saw me, but he seemed to know I needed space.

What I really wanted was to stay home with Maxi. But my parents were right; I couldn't stay home with her for weeks. They agreed when things got nearer *the end*, we'd take turns staying with her.

I did stay home with her whenever I wasn't in school. And Abby came over to visit us most days. The vet had said we should make sure Maxi took it easy as much as possible so as not to risk fracturing her leg with the cancer.

When Rory heard what was going on, he came right over. Man, the big guy was crushed.

"Not Maxi!" he yelled. "We need a second opinion."

"We already got a second opinion," I said.

"Then a third one."

"It won't change anything, Rory. It is what it is. There's nothing we can do."

Nothing!

So that's what I did—nothing! Put one foot in front of the other each day.

"Timminy, I know you're sad about Maxi," Abby said to me one afternoon. "I am too. But Maxi needs more than a zombie Timminy for the rest of her life."

"Easy for you to say, Abby."

"No, it's not."

"Yes, it is. You have your guide dog coming. And all I have to look forward to is a *dead* dog. Heck, Abby, why'd you make me read all those dead dog books anyway? Marley, Sounder, Old Yeller—they all died. And now I get a real dead dog, not just one in a book. Thanks."

Abby didn't say anything.

"What's the matter? Hard to face the truth?"

"No, it's hard for you to face the truth, Timminy."

"Shut up. Just shut up."

She did shut up. Then stared at me. I know she's blind and can't really stare. But she *did*. The whites of her eyes froze in place. It felt like ghost eyes looking right at me. Maxi would soon be a ghost just like those eyes.

"Abby, I *hate* you."

I gasped. I didn't mean that, but it popped out.

"I hate everybody."

"Let it out," Abby said.

"I can't," I cried. "If I let it out, I don't know if I'll have anything left inside. My heart's already been ripped out. What happens when Maxi is dead for real, and I don't have any heart left to feel with? This STINKS! My life STINKS! Maxi's dying STINKS."

I screamed and screamed and screamed until I was all screamed out.

Abby was still there.

"Feel a little better?" she asked.

"No!"

"So keep screaming."

I tried. "It's NOT, NOT, NOT, NOT, NOT . . . FAIR!"

Then I sobbed and sobbed.

And Abby was still there.

I wiped my eyes with both hands, but my face was

still wet. "Why are you still here listening?" I asked. "Don't you want to tell me to shut my face and stop feeling sorry for myself? You've always been good at that, Abby."

Abby reached out to wipe some of the tears off my face, tears she couldn't see, but she could feel even though *I* was the one crying them. She said, "I'm here because I'm your friend. And this time, Timminy, you have every right to feel sorry for yourself because Maxi is dying and that STINKS!"

Together we yelled, "STINKS! STINKS! STINKS! STINKS! STINKS!"

It felt like something inside me burst, or maybe it was more that it had released and I didn't have to hold things in anymore.

I sighed. And Abby sat with me in my silence.

My breathing calmed.

My heart slowed.

My tears dried.

I sighed once more and said, "Abby, it makes no sense. How can one dog have so much stupid *bad* luck? Deaf, and now cancer. It's not fair."

Abby reached for my arm, found it, and held on. "You're right. It isn't fair. But another question is . . . How can one dog who's deaf and has cancer have such stupid *good* luck to find you out of all the boys in the world to be her boy?"

I stared at Abby, then whispered, "You're half right. I'm the one with stupid good luck to have found Maxi. No matter for how long."

So that's what I decided to do that day and every day. Hang on to Maxi and our stupid good luck.

SECRET #46
Hold on to the good parts for as long as you can.

CHAPTER 47

MAXI SEEMED BETTER, happier too, once I stopped acting like she was *already* dead. She'd be dead sooner than was fair, sooner than I wanted. Heck, we'd all be dead someday. But we weren't dead now. We were alive—even Maxi. It was time to live.

And we did.

I still was sad and angry at times, but not all the time. Not even most of the time.

After a blizzard when we had a day off from school, we made an igloo with snow and water. We packed it in, dug it out, shaped it. Rory was our construction foreman, since he'd made one before. It was big enough for all of us to get in at once. Everyone had to bend over inside since the ceiling was low, except for Maxi and me. We stood tall and proud and made the others jealous.

We wanted an igloo sleepover since it was surprisingly warm inside. But the Boss wouldn't hear of it and used Maxi as her excuse: "Maxi's bones ache enough without having to sleep on cold, hard-packed snow." The Boss won that one.

Actually, Maxi won that one. I didn't want to spend a single night away from her. We'd figured out heat *did* make Maxi feel better. So we heated rice bags for her to snuggle with when she crawled in bed and under the covers with me. When she was on her own dog bed, we tucked a fuzzy fleece blanket around her to help keep her warm.

Every Friday night we had a pizza party. At first, Maxi walked around the room from person to person flashing her puppy-dog eyes to get sympathy, but mostly to get crusts, everyone's pizza crusts. Later, when it was harder for her to walk, we'd put her bed in the middle of the room and we'd all sit in a circle around her and bring her our pizza crusts so she didn't have to get up. (And don't tell Mom, but I have the feeling she knew all along that Maxi got more than crusts—pepperoni, ham, bacon, and cheese too. She must have gotten lots of cheese 'cause her Friday-night after-pizza-party farts were the *stinkiest evah*—as Abby said).

For Christmas, we spoiled Maxi at a doggie spa. When she was finished, she looked like a beanbag chair made of dandelion fuzz wearing a big red bow. She was so pretty we took lots of family photos of her first, her only Christmas. Rory was in charge of the photos. Dad and some neighbors had hired him to help shovel snow—so Rory had saved enough money to buy that camera and lens he'd wanted.

He took photos of Maxi in front of our Christmas tree, sitting next to her Christmas stocking hanging from the mantel, plus outside on top of a big snow bank— Queen of the Mountain! Rory carried her up. She barked like crazy up on top as if to say, "I'm the BOSS now, Mama Harris—take that!"

The best photo was one of Rory, Maxi, and me. And Abby took it! Rory had set up his camera on top of a stool (the best tripod he could find). He'd shown Abby hand over hand which button to push and how to squeeze it slowly so it would auto-focus. He told Abby he'd snap his fingers when we were ready and then all she had to do was push the button. She did. Just one take. And when we saw it uploaded onto my computer, we agreed it was the best photo of the whole shoot— perfect expressions, all looking at the camera, and centered just so. We ribbed Abby that instead of a librarian she could become the world's most famous *blind* photographer.

Rory took more photos whenever he came over (and he came over a lot), but my favorite photos were taken in the spring. Maxi was in more pain and having a harder time getting around. But one day, on the first really nice spring day, Maxi seemed so happy—like she was a puppy again. She found the last small patch of snow on the lawn and squatted and peed on it as if to say, "Take *that*, winter!"

Then she limped from smell to smell on the lawn and buried her snout deep each time as if the smell of mud was the best smell in the world. But then she found a *better* one, and finally the *best* one. She rubbed her head, her neck, and then rolled in it to savor the smell. But when she stood up, I saw it was more than a smell.

"Ew! What did you get into, Maxi?" I rubbed her fur to remove the greenish-brown spots, but they seemed to explode and smear all over.

"Ew! It's the stinkiest smell!" I looked at my hands and at Maxi and stepped back. Then she went back to sniffing and rolling in it, so delighted and proud of herself.

Rory, who had been clicking photo after photo of Maxi, burst out laughing. "Jackpot, Maxi!" he said.

Abby was there too. "What is it? A skunk?"

"Ew! It doesn't smell like a skunk—it's worse than a skunk. Here, smell." I went over to Abby and stuck my hands in front of her face.

"Ew! Ew! Ew!" She gagged.

Rory was still laughing, but snap-snapping photos at the same time—of my hands, and Abby's reaction, and Maxi as she tried to bury herself in that greenish-brown stinky sludge.

I ran at Rory with my slimy hands and yelled, "Stop laughing. Stop taking pictures. Help us. What the heck is this? If you don't help, I'm gonna rub this through your hair."

Rory laughed louder than ever. "Luckily you can't reach my hair without a stepladder, Minny. And it's a little poop."

"What?" I gasped.

"You got yourself some wild turkey poop! A dime-sized plop can spread to the size of a watermelon if you touch it, and it's stinkier than a whole gym full of babies with dirty diapers."

Abby burst out laughing, and eventually I did too. And Maxi kept rolling in the stuff while Rory took photos. For once the Beast of the East didn't come to my rescue. I had to get out the washtub and hose and suds Maxi up before my parents got home. I wouldn't let Abby help since she couldn't see where the turkey poop was. Rory didn't lift a finger to help, but he captured it all on film.

SECRET #47

When life gives you a pile of poop, you're gonna get dirty—so you may as well roll with it.

CHAPTER 48

THERE WERE LOTS of signs from Maxi that it was getting nearer the end.

We had to move my mattress to the floor since she couldn't jump up on it anymore.

Her back legs started to give out.

There were days when she wouldn't eat at all.

I still wasn't sure when we'd be sure. Vets and people we knew, who'd had their pets put down, said, "You'll just know."

But I wasn't sure I'd let myself know. And my parents wanted it to be my decision. But, heck, I was a kid, a *little* kid. I wasn't ready to play God. So I watched Maxi, looking into her eyes, waiting for her to decide, for her to tell me it was time.

And, finally, she did.

She could barely climb the stairs up to my bedroom. But she wanted to. She needed to. It was her job to guard me at night. Dad and I helped her up by standing behind her on the stairs and lifting her backside so she could go up a step at a time. But one night her front legs gave out too. Somehow we made it up.

Maxi slept so soundly that night, the best in weeks. The next morning she stood at the top of the stairs and knew she couldn't get down. We knew helping her down was more dangerous than helping her up. She weighed almost ninety-five pounds.

She couldn't stay upstairs all day—even if I stayed home with her. We called Rory, and he came over to help Dad carry her downstairs—one holding her in front and the other in back. Maxi didn't squirm. She seemed to know they were helping her. I could see the pain in her eyes.

She hurt.

All the way to her bones.

Even her pride.

Every inch.

She hurt.

I held my hand up when they got to the bottom of the stairs and said, "Load her in the car. It's time."

"Are you sure?" asked Dad.

"I'm not ready," said Rory.

"But she is, Rory."

"I didn't bring my camera."

"That's okay. No photos today—this isn't how she wants us to remember her."

Rory tried to swallow a sob. But he was too big. His sobs were too big to swallow. I didn't have any words to make him feel better. So I patted him on the back. Pats had always made Maxi feel better.

I opened the hatchback and spread out Maxi's fuzzy fleece blanket, and my dad and Rory gently loaded her in.

Then I left Rory with Maxi to say their good-byes.

Mom called Mrs. Winslow to bring Abby over for her good-bye.

I ran inside and grabbed some cheese.

Abby asked the same question. "Are you sure?"

"*She's* sure, Abby."

Abby hugged me first. Her whole body quivered. And then she leaned into the back of the car and hugged Maxi and sobbed into her fur. She wasn't calming down so I gently pulled her back and said, "It's time, Abby."

She turned to me and said, "You're the brave one, Timminy."

I didn't feel brave, I just felt sure.

I climbed into the back with Maxi. No seat belts back there, but Mom didn't say a word, and I knew if we got stopped by a cop for breaking the seat belt law, they'd have to answer to the Boss.

I said, "Put down all the windows, Dad, and let's take

the back roads to the vet's." He did, and Maxi twitched her nose, taking in every last country smell (I hoped one would be turkey poop). I fed her small bites of cheese and she licked my hands not because they tasted like cheese, but because I was her boy.

At the vet's, Dad went in first. The vet assistants came out to help carry Maxi.

We gently lifted her in her blanket. Mom and Dad held on to an edge of the blanket. Me too.

I only remember a couple of things after we carried her in. I just wanted to be with Maxi the way she had always been there for me.

The vet said something about ashes and a paw print and fur clippings to remember her by. I spoke up and said, "Lots of fur, please."

The vet explained what would happen when he gave her the shot, but I didn't hear him. (Later, my parents said he'd told us she might still twitch after it was over, after she'd been still for a while, but it would just be a nerve letting go—she'd already be gone. But I didn't hear that. And he didn't know Maxi the way I knew Maxi.)

I *do* remember hugging and holding Maxi when it happened. She was on her blanket on the floor. I sat next to her, my parents kneeling behind me, each with a hand on one of my shoulders. But then their hands started to quiver. I could tell they were crying for Maxi, for me, for themselves. Their quivering hands made my shoulders shake. And it would have been so easy to catch the rhythm of their sadness, but I refused. It took all my strength to absorb their quivers and not let *my* body shake.

I didn't want the last thing Maxi felt to be sadness. I only wanted her to feel love. So I wouldn't let their quivers move past my elbows. I willed my forearms and my hands to be strong and give loving pats and send love, only love, through my fingers to Maxi.

Until.

She.

Stopped.

Moving.

Then finally I leaned down and put my forehead against hers.

"I love you, girl. I love you."

Then Maxi (they can call it a spasm or whatever they want, but I know better) leaned in to me. Her head slipped off my forehead and into my chest as she gave me one final Maxi hug. That's what I felt.

That's what I *know*.

SECRET #48
All that matters is LOVE.

CHAPTER 49

SECRET #49
Sometimes there are no words.

CHAPTER 50

ALL I REMEMBERED was the silence. It was so *loud*—like the air was humming or buzzing. Had it been like that for Maxi? In her silence? In her deafness? Maybe it was so loud because there was no Maxi snoring or eating or walking or barking or anything.

A life makes noise. Maxi's life made a lot of noise and now there was a giant buzzing emptiness.

At first, I tried to be polite when people said things about Maxi dying. But then I gave up. When someone said, "You can always get another dog," I wanted to scream, "There was only ONE Maxi!"

When people said, "I know how you feel," I wanted to head-butt them—because no one, *no one* had been Maxi's boy, so they couldn't know how I felt.

And it's stupid to have rules about how long you're allowed to cry and when you're supposed to flip a switch and stop crying. You can't even think. All you can do is feel. So how the heck are you supposed to follow rules?

And who made up those rules anyway? So I made my own rules, ones I thought Maxi would have liked.

Everything Maxi stayed Maxi. Her food dish stayed in the same spot, her bed stayed in the same place, her toys in her toy basket. Even her last pile of poop on the lawn was going to stay there until it blended back into the ground. I liked all those reminders of her. Somehow she felt closer, like she'd always be part of my life.

And she would be.

On the first weekend after Maxi died, I invited all our friends to a pizza party. We left our crusts on her bed in the middle of the room. I'd divided that big bag of Maxi fur they'd given us at the vet's into smaller plastic bags and gave some of her fur to each friend with a note attached. I pretended Maxi had written them.

Like Rory's . . .

Rory,
Thanks for saving me from a porcupine quill infection. And for the all the photos—you'll never find another puppy as photogenic as me. Keep nagging your dad to get a dog 'cause you're a dog kinda guy.

Your friend,
Little Beast

P.S. I promise not to tell the world your secret
that you're more a marshmallow than a beast.

Rory surprised me by showing a slide show with all
of Maxi's photos. We ran it through and through on our
big-screen TV. Then he played the turkey poop video
he'd taken, and it almost felt like Maxi was with us . . .

"Ew! That's worse than milk snot," squealed Devon.

"Did someone cut the cheese in here? Or does this
Maxi video have a sniff-and-whiff option?"

"GROSS OUT!"

We all laughed and laughed. Maxi made us laugh—
once more.

After Rory, Devon, Becca, Brian, Benjamin, Kassy,
and Carver all left, it was just me and Abby.

I told her, "When you get your guide dog, I want to
take a special walk. It might be a while before I'm ready
though. And when we walk, I'm going to take my Maxi
fur and ashes along. I'll let your dog smell Maxi's fur so
they can get to know each other. Then we'll leave a trail
of Maxi's ashes in the woods."

Abby was crying, quiet crying. "Why the woods?"
she asked.

"Because she loved it there even though she didn't get
to go very often. Because that's where she was a hero.
Because there are so many smells in the woods—and all

kinds of delicious poop too. That's where we're gonna set her free, Abby."

SECRET #50
Some things in life are so big, you couldn't forget them even if you wanted to—and you *won't* want to.

CHAPTER 51

ONE NIGHT, MAXI came to me.

In a dream.

Or maybe I was awake.

I couldn't be sure.

Her face appeared, the reverse of fading out, she faded in. First, a white blur like fuzzy Christmas tree lights when you squint your eyes. Then, she slowly came into focus. If I shut my eyes tight, she disappeared and my world was still a black hole. But when I relaxed, loosened my eyes, she became clearer, came closer.

She looked so happy. So happy to see me again.

Me too, girl, me too.

Then her big, furry body filled my eyes, filled my head. It was like being in the front row of an IMAX movie theater. She covered the whole screen. Her tail wagged, which triggered her body waggling. I laughed. She cocked her head to the side, looking puzzled. That made me laugh even harder. She barked, then stopped, as if waiting for me. So I laughed again. When I stopped, she barked.

My turn. I laughed.

Her turn. She barked.

I laughed.

She barked.

I cried.

You can hear, girl. You can hear now!

I checked. To be sure.

Sit, Maxi.

She sat without a sign language cue.

Give me a kiss, girl.

And she did. A big, fat, slobbery kiss.

How you doing, girl? I've missed you.

Maxi *woof*ed and *woof*ed, jumped this way and that way, as if she were telling me a story of all she'd been up to. She was so excited, so happy. Then she leaned in to give me one of her hugs with her head pressing against me, but this time it almost felt like she had arms, or wings, as they closed around me and held me. Held my body, reached in, and held my heart too.

I smiled and cried, all at the same time.

Maxi pulled back and stared at me, deep, past my eyes, to the inside. She was saying her final good-bye.

One more slurpy kiss, then she turned and ran off. She left as fast, as mysteriously, as she'd appeared.

I shouted after her, "I'll always remember you, girl. ALWAYS."

I couldn't move for the longest time. I wasn't thinking, just being. I wanted to lock that Maxi feeling inside me, to never let it go.

When I finally could move, I had no idea what time it was. It was like time didn't exist.

I knew I wouldn't tell Mom or Dad about Maxi coming to visit. I think it would make them sad, sad for me. But I wasn't as sad anymore. Maxi made me feel better, like she'd always made me feel better.

There was someone, though, that I *had* to tell about Maxi's visit.

I got off my bed. It was dark, a moonless night. Still, I didn't turn on the light. I didn't need to. I finally understood it was possible to feel your way through this world. I sat at my desk, felt for the power button on my computer, turned it on. I went to FaceTime and called Abby.

It took her a while to answer. When she did, I clicked the audio only option. I didn't need to see her. I just wanted to hear her, as she had always heard me. Her voice would tell me everything I needed to know.

"Timminy, it's the middle of the night. I was sleeping. Is everything okay?"

"Yes, sorry. I just needed to tell you a couple of things."

Abby paused, not wanting to step on what I had to say.

"Maxi came to see me tonight."

"A dream?" she asked.

"More than a dream," I said. "And guess what? She could *hear*."

"Oh, Timminy, Maxi could always hear you."

"I know, Abby, like you can always *see* me."

I could feel Abby's smile in the darkness.

"I'm ready," I said.

Abby waited.

"I want to go for our walk."

"Now?" asked Abby.

"In the morning, after breakfast."

Abby paused. I could hear all the hope in that pause.

I said, "Yes, Abby Winslow, I'm finally ready to go for a walk in the woods with you and that guide dog of yours."

Then, on cue, a bark filled the air—a small bark, Darshan's bark.

I smiled and said, "Sounds like Darshan is ready. You haven't gone in the woods yet, have you?"

"No, we've been waiting for you."

"I'm ready."

"I'm glad," said Abby.

I smiled—I hoped Abby could feel my smile in the darkness. Then I said, "Um, by the way, do you know if

MIRA trained Darshan to signal you to duck when you're walking under trees?"

"I'm not sure," said Abby. "That's why you're coming with us."

"Just so you know, Abby, I'm out of practice. So you'd better hang on to your eyeballs."

Abby laughed.

I laughed.

We laughed together.

That's what *best friends* do.

SECRET #51

Best friends are forever friends. They make you laugh and cry and laugh some more—even the ones who have moved on.

SPECIAL THANKS

There would be no Maxi without Maggie, my "favorite puppy in the whole wide world—all time, ever" (as I used to tell her). Our beloved Maggie, who was black, not white; an Irish setter mix, not a Great Pyrenees; who could hear some, but listened rarely; who lived much longer than Maxi, to be almost fourteen (in human years). She shared her porcupine-quill and turkey-poo adventures. She taught me her secrets and showed me how to say good-bye when *she* was ready. Then Maggie led me to Maxi's story as she sat on my desk each day (her photo, her ashes, her fur sample). I always said you were a great author's dog, Maggie, as you lay by my chair while I wrote all those years. Little did I know, girl, you had one more gift for me—this story. I owe you big-time the next time we meet. I'm thinking a mountain of horseradish cheese for starters.

My next thanks goes to my first reader, always my first reader, my husband, Paul Knowles. When we married more than thirty years ago, I had a dream—to become a children's book author. You believed in my dream, always. You believed when I collected hundreds and hundreds of rejections for thirteen years before getting my first picture book published. Most of all, you know who I am at my core, and you have always guided me to write from my heart, from my soul. You have made me a better author and, more important, a better person. I am so grateful you are my forever love.

Thanks to my agent, Susan Cohen, at Writers House, who has always believed in me and my writing. Sue, you have been so positive and encouraging through years of revisions and rejections (and some acceptances along the way too). This author journey I'm on truly has felt like "ours"—the highs, the lows, the laughter, the tears. I am honored to share it with you.

I owe a huge thanks to Nora Long, Susan Cohen's assistant at Writers House. Nora read an early version of this manuscript and had the most amazing reader's eye to know exactly what it needed. She wrote me a six-page, detailed editorial letter encouraging me, challenging me, and guiding me through a major revision that would then be ready for submission.

I can't thank my editor and publisher, Nancy Paulsen, enough for saying *yes* to Maxi, for adopting this crazy dog and this newbie middle-grade author. I wanted Susan Cohen to submit *Maxi's Secrets* to Nancy because I had read her books and knew she published books with "heart." I hoped the story I wrote from my heart would touch her heart. And when Sue Cohen called on June 4, 2015 (of course I know the date), to tell me Nancy Paulsen wanted to publish *Maxi's Secrets*, I sobbed, tears of joy. Then it felt like Nancy was hugging me the whole way through the revision process—her comments included squeals of delight when she read a part she loved, wise questions as she encouraged me to go deeper into the story, and magical powers as she helped me to somehow write "more" while writing "less" (thirteen thousand words less in the end). Nancy, I thank you from the bottom of my heart for your "heart."

And, finally, this book is better thanks to the experts who shared their wisdom with me. Thanks to literacy strategist Susan Dee and librarian Cathy Potter for their "nerdy" book wisdom and suggestions. Thanks to veterinarian Bill Bryant for being our Maggie's favorite vet and for giving me guidance on the canine medical information in this book. Thanks to Christina Lee, founder and president of Deaf Dogs Rock (deafdogsrock.com), for sharing her wisdom and advice on deaf dog issues. Thanks to Chad Hill, a seventh-grade student who is blind, and Jude Carey, a teacher of the visually impaired, for their detailed and thoughtful feedback and suggestions on how to make Abby's blindness ring true. Thanks also to copy editors Anne Heausler and Robert Farren, who taught me some writing tricks and gave this novel the final polish it needed.

Lynn Plourde